THE ACCIDENTAL ADVENTURES OF ONION O'BRIEN

—

THE GREAT APE ESCAPE

JASON BYRNE

ILLUSTRATED BY OISÍN McGANN

GILL BOOKS

Gill Books
Hume Avenue
Park West
Dublin 12
www.gillbooks.ie

Gill Books is an imprint of M.H. Gill & Co.

Text © Jason Byrne 2018, 2019
Illustrations © Oisín McGann 2018, 2019
First published in hardback 2018
This paperback edition published 2019

978 0 7171 8488 0

Edited by Oisín McGann
Printed by ScandBook, Sweden

This book is typeset in Nimrod.

A CIP catalogue record for this book is available from the British Library.

5 4 3 2 1

FOR DEVIN AND DANIEL, YOU'RE MY WORLD

Jason Byrne is one of Ireland's most popular comedians and a judge on Virgin Media One's *Ireland's Got Talent*. He has a huge international career as a stand-up comedian and many television credits to his name, including *Wild Things* on Sky One. *The Accidental Adventures of Onion O'Brien: The Great Ape Escape* is the first of his series of brilliantly funny children's books, inspired by his own childhood misadventures. The second in the series, *The Head of Ned Belly*, is published in autumn 2019.

Oisín McGann is a writer and illustrator who has produced dozens of books, including *Headbomz: Wreckin' Yer Head*, the *Mad Grandad series*, *The Forbidden Files*, as well as a whole bunch of critically acclaimed novels.

CHAPTER ONE:
—
A RUN-IN WITH THE LAW

H ere they were, running from the police, and it was only the start of the weekend. It wasn't like they'd done anything serious, Onion thought to himself as he struggled to keep up with his three friends. It was pretty stupid really. Sure, the government wanted them to spend half their lives in school, but sneak onto school property when it was closed? Oh no – that was *trespassing*.

'Onion, pick up . . . pick up the pace, man!' Dallan panted from up ahead. Dallan might have been shorter than his friend, but he was a lot faster. 'He's gainin' on yeh!'

Onion was too scared to look back. Dallan and Sive were out in front, belting across the football pitch, with Onion and Clíona trying hard to match their speed. They were four of the gang known as the Five O's, and they were in trouble. Again.

Behind the four trespassers, Garda Fergus Plunkett, known to the local kids as 'The Ferg', was pounding after them in hot pursuit. The Ferg was not a popular man, either in the Dublin suburb of Ballinlud or with his own colleagues in the Gardaí. The other guards considered this blustery loudmouth an embarrassment to the uniform. A blocky body on stumpy legs, he was a brute of a man, with a moustache plonked like a brush across his steaming red face. He was out of shape, and the effort to catch the young trespassers was making him even more furious than when he'd started out. And he was furious for half the time he was awake. He spent a large part of his life in a state of furiousness.

'Next . . . next time I tell you to . . . to hide,' Sive growled back at Onion . . . you better . . . flumpin' **HIDE!**'

'I know, I know, I'm . . . I'm sorry,' Onion wheezed.

As usual, this was his fault. When the Garda car showed up outside the school, everyone else had dived into the hedge between the schoolyard and the church. Onion had frozen. He'd stayed right where he was, standing out on the grass in full view like a complete guzzer.

The inhaler for his asthma was bouncing on his chest now, hanging from a cord around his neck for easy access – something his granny insisted on. Every now and then it flew up and whacked him on the face, so he grabbed it to keep it still and urged more acceleration out of his long, thin white legs.

He was sweating like crazy too. It was pouring down through his red hair and soaking through his hand-me-down clothes. His glasses were sliding down his damp nose with all the jolting.

'Stop in the name of The Ferg ... I mean the law! Stop, you little hooligans! Stop before I have a heart attack! Heh ... heh ... please stop!' The Ferg wheezed.

Onion's legs nearly gave way when he thought about getting caught. If The Ferg found out where he lived, he'd tell Onion's granny and grandad what he'd been doing. Granny would completely lose the head. Aw, jaypers. She'd go out of her mind. Oh no, oh no, oh no . . .

'RUN FOR YOUR LIVES!'

CHAPTER ONE: A RUN-IN WITH THE LAW

Sive howled, and surged ahead in a mad spurt of speed, her tall dark spikes of hair bending back in the wind.

Clíona, who was running just ahead of Onion, glanced back at The Ferg with panic on her pale brown face. She'd be in the most trouble if they were caught. She was almost as rubbish at running as Onion was, and looked it, with her usual baggy combats, oversized shirt and T-shirt all flapping around her. Her long hair was bound in a bandanna, but it still bounced all over the place. The big pocket on the left leg of her combats was swinging heavily, knocking against her. In that pocket was Clíona's latest invention.

The plan had been to test the gadget out on the church bell. Now, they were probably going to go to prison or, worse, forced to stay in with Grandad and listen to his stories about being in the army he was never actually in. Onion wasn't sure what kind of punishment the guards could use against children these days.

Top Five Punishments from the Guards

1. Learn the safe cross code in English

2. Learn the safe cross code in Irish

3. Extra Mass

4. Toilet-cleaning duty (number ones and twos)

5. Actual prison

He wanted to cry, but he needed all his energy for running.

His foot caught on a ridge of grass and he nearly fell on his face. Flailing his arms, he managed to keep his balance and keep going. As well as his glasses, Onion had a patch over his left eye. This was because he had a wonky eye. The patch wasn't over his *bad* eye, which would have made sense. No, it was over his *good* eye, the left one, that actually did what his brain told it to. The doctor's thinking was that, if they made his wonky one do all the work, it would have to start behaving itself.

CHAPTER ONE: A RUN-IN WITH THE LAW

Needless to say, having an eye with a mind of its own could cause all sorts of problems, especially when you were running from the guards.

Sive was the first to reach the gate out onto the road. What none of the Five O's had realised was that as they'd booted it across the football pitch, The Ferg's partner had simply turned the car around and coasted back down the road to the other gate. Now, she pulled up, opened her door and stood up, waiting for them. Garda Bridie Judge was younger than The Ferg; small, fit and tough-looking, with short-cut blonde hair. She was all business. Sive spotted the trap and veered off to the right, starting back across the field in another direction, determined that the guards would never take her alive. Clíona was already splitting off to the left, slow but steady, no doubt calculating the exact angle that would enable her to escape from both guards.

As Dallan stumbled the last few metres to the gate, he turned the walk into a casual saunter, waved to the guard and leaned on the gate like there was nowhere else he'd rather be.

'Good morning, Garda!' he greeted her in a bright voice with a warm smile. He gestured to the three other children in various positions around the football pitch. 'My friends and I were just out for our morning run. Healthy for the body and mind! Always a pleasure to trade a few words with a guardian of the peace. And such a *strikingly attractive* one too! I see you're driving the latest Ford Mondeo patrol vehicle. Does that come with leather seats as standard. . . ?'

'Spare me the smart mouth, little boy,' Judge said in a bored voice. 'Zip it or lose it.'

Dallan wasn't sure what that threat meant, but her tone was enough to shut him up.

Onion didn't even make it to the gate. He collapsed onto the grass, gasping for breath, and took a quick puff from his inhaler. Coming up on his knees, he held up his hands and cried out in despair:

'I did it, I mean I didn't do it, they did it, I mean they didn't do it, somebody did it and it wasn't them, us, I mean meeeeeeeeee eeeeeee ...' Onion whimpered to himself.

'What's your name, boy?' asked Judge.

'It's Onion, sir, er, ma'am . . . I mean Garda.'

'Don't mess with me, lad. Your real name! Do you think I was born yesterday?'

'No, Garda. My name really is Onion, and I don't think you were born yesterday. You look very old.'

Judge raised an eyebrow at Onion, a flush of anger rising in her cheeks.

'I mean young! You look very young, like a baby. But not one that was born yesterday. Please have mercy!'

'No one is called Onion,' said Judge.

'I am, I swear. When I was born my dad thought I had a head like an onion, and every time someone looked at me I made them cry, just like an onion does.'

'And I suppose your name is Carrot?' she asked Dallan.

Just as Dallan opened his mouth to reply, Garda Fergus Plunket staggered up, breathing like a man who'd just been pushed out of the airlock of a spaceship. Bridie Judge glared at her fellow officer in disgust. She had joined the Garda Síochána because of her love of action and automatic weapons. Chasing a bunch of loser kids across a field was not her idea of fighting crime, especially if those kids were named after vegetables.

'Fergus, we've gotta go!' she barked. 'We got a call. Someone's just robbed the McDonald's. They're heading our way. They're heavily armed and viciously dangerous. Finally, some proper villains!'

'I'll be along in a minute,' The Ferg said, heaving in breaths. 'I just want to give these kids a piece of my mind.'

'You don't have much to spare, Plunkett,' she told him. 'And I need what little you have. Get in the car, let's go take down some gangstas.'

With great reluctance, The Ferg gave up on the four 'hooligans', lumbered through the gate, and climbed stiffly into the car's passenger seat. Having seen what was going on, Dallan and Sive had stopped running. Now, they made their way back towards the gate. Bridie Judge cast a hard stare around at the four Five O's.

'Behave yourselves, kids. Stay in school,' she said. Then, thinking, she added, '. . . when it's open. When it's *not* open, stay *out* of school. Don't mess with me on this. I am the law.'

And with that, she put on a pair of mirror sunglasses, got into the car and revved the engine.

She did a skid-turn that spun the car out onto the road before roaring away, the sirens wailing.

Clíona flopped against the gate, sighing with relief. Dallan came up behind them, pushing his designer glasses back up his nose. Unlike Onion, he was merely short-sighted – though he was *seriously* short-sighted. Tutting at the creases in his expensive shirt, he brushed his fingers through his footballer's hairstyle to clear out the bits of hedge that were stuck there. Sive was there too now, in her usual pose, chewing gum as she stuck her hands into the pockets of her hoodie. She stared after the departing Garda car, smiling slightly and trembling from the adrenalin rush.

'That was lucky,' she said. 'Saved by an armed robbery. That was *really* lucky.'

'Yeah,' Dallan agreed. 'It worked though, right? Clíona? The test worked?'

'I think it might even work from here,' Clíona replied. She took the small black box from her combats pocket and held it up. 'Listen.'

She pointed it at the steeple of the Holy Mary Mother of God Church, just beyond the school building. Then she pressed the button on the box, and in the distance, they heard the church bell start ringing. Clíona had managed to copy the signal that the priest used to activate the bell.

'Cool,' Sive said, grinning.

'Yeah, that's sweet.' Dallan agreed. Then he looked around and shook his head in dismay. 'Onion, what . . . ? Aw jaypers. You can get off your knees now, you eejit. And put your hands down!'

CHAPTER TWO:
—
BACK IN THE 1980S

When Onion got home, it was a little after eleven in the morning, but Grandad Paddy was already in his usual place in the living room on a Saturday, sitting in his armchair, his bare feet in a basin of hot water. Nothing was visible apart from his legs and his hands because he was behind his newspaper. He wouldn't come out from behind that paper for a couple of hours.

Onion's little sister, Molly, was off playing in a friend's house. His older brother, Derek, the fifth member of the Five O's, was at football training. The gang's name came from their surnames: Sive O'Connor, Dallan Okoye, Clíona O'Hare and

Onion O'Brien. Derek was included as a member, though he always said he wasn't part of their stupid gang.

Granny Mary was sitting at the kitchen table, knitting a sock, timing a pie she had baking in the oven and shaking her head in disgust at something a politician was saying on the radio. Onion went to walk into the kitchen, but his foot didn't even touch the lino before Granny's voice stopped him dead.

'Do not set your foot, or even feet, near that good lino – I've only detached the tea towels from my knees. It's the only way to get a floor proper shiny, scrub it with tea towels on your knees.'

'Why can't you just use a mop, Granny?' asked Onion.

'You know the story about the mop, Onion. Grandad got his hands on it,' answered Granny. 'Now get yourself a nice carrot stick from the fridge there, but lean in and get it – don't stand on that floor.'

Carrot sticks? Onion nearly gagged. He was about to start arguing with her but stopped himself. Because if he talked too much, Granny would notice he was a bit stressed, and then she'd ask why, and Onion was completely useless at keeping secrets. His wonky eye (she called it his 'special' eye) always went haywire when he lied. So he might end up blurting out the whole story of trespassing on school property to get close to the church without being seen to test Clíona's church-bell remote control. And then he'd tell her about getting chased by the guards.

And then Granny would throw a wobbler and haul him off down to the church for confession.

So, keep it cool, he told himself. Besides, today was a special day, and he didn't want to ruin it.

'Here, what time are we going to the circus?' he asked.

Granny put the half-finished sock down on her lap and looked at him. She was a stern oul' one, but he loved her dearly. Her curly, greying brown hair grew up in a kind of lop-sided tower over a long, kind face lined by hard work and bother. She gave him a 'how many times to I have to say this' smile.

'Oh my God, I've said seven o'clock at least seven times,' Granny said. 'Seven o'clock. The show starts at seven o'clock. Now that's nine times, and saying seven nine times isn't good for your health. Make sure your friends are here by a quarter to.'

You might wonder why Onion and his brother and sister lived with their grandparents instead of their mother and father. The fact of the matter was their parents had disappeared some years before in mysterious circumstances.

But that is another story for another time.

'Sure, they'll be here anyway,' Onion replied.

This was true. The Five O's tended to hang out in Onion's house. There were two reasons for this. First, Granny loved baking, so if you hung around long enough, you were bound to get a warm scone or a piece of sponge cake or pie, because people who enjoyed baking stuff needed people who enjoyed eating baked stuff. This was a service the gang were happy to provide.

Second – and this was the main reason – Granny Mary and Grandad Paddy had raised their own kids back in the 1980s, when parenting was very different. They weren't like twenty-first-century parents. Their approach to supervising children was to not supervise them very much at all. Okay, Onion's sister was only little and needed a bit of attention, but Onion and Derek and their friends could go hours at a time without their grandparents wondering where they were and what might be happening to them. Dangerous roads, hazardous waste-ground, a complete lack of health and safety – these were all considered a necessary part of growing up, as far as Grandad Paddy and Granny Mary were concerned. Or, rather, not concerned at all.

This was perfect for the Five O's because it meant the others could say they were going over to Onion's house, so they were off the hook with their own parents, and then the gang could pretty much do whatever they wanted – just as long as they showed their faces every few hours so Granny could see they were still alive and give them a scone.

And now they were going to the circus that had come to the Dublin suburb of Ballinlud. Onion went up to his small room in their very ordinary three-bed semi-detached house. Opening his window, he was able to crane his neck and just see the Big Top on the green at the end of the road. He'd already been up to check it out with the others, watching it all get set up.

Tonight was the opening show and Grandad had got free tickets for the whole gang through some lad in the hardware shop – probably a present for all the nails and hammers he'd bought over the years. Onion was buzzing with excitement. He'd never been to a real circus, and this was supposed to be the top one in Ireland.

They boasted they had one of the world's greatest acrobats, The Great Orangini. People said he could do things no human should be able to do. He was a mysterious figure too. He was never seen in public without his famous clown costume and make-up. In a world where celebrities had their whole lives on the web, hardly anyone knew what The Great Orangini really looked like. That was cool.

He could be out there right now, walking around, Onion thought, and nobody would know.

'Granny! I'm goin' out again!' he roared as he charged down the stairs.

CHAPTER TWO: BACK IN THE 1980S

'Stop shouting through the house!' she roared back. 'And don't go far – I'm doing lunch in an hour. And pick up Molly on your way back! Now I'm shouting through the house! Stop making me shout through the house at you, Onion!'

But Onion was already out the front door and jogging up the road to where the circus people were still setting up for the evening's show. He was wondering if you could tell someone was a world-class acrobat just by looking at them and whether he might be lucky enough to spot The Great Orangini.

CHAPTER THREE:
—
THE GREAT ORANGINI

They were all psyched up for this: Onion and Sive and Dallan and Clíona and big brother Derek, the moody thirteen-year-old, and little Molly and Granny Mary. They all stood in the hall, and out in the porch, waiting for Grandad Paddy, who had decided he needed to go to the loo just as they were heading out the door.

'May I say, you're looking splendid this evening, Mrs O'Brien,' Dallan said in a smooth voice, looking over his glasses at Granny.

'And you're sounding like a chancer, Dallan,' Granny replied. 'But thanks all the same.'

'Pleb,' Sive muttered under her breath as she elbowed Dallan in the ribs.

CHAPTER THREE: THE GREAT ORANGINI

When Grandad Paddy emerged from the toilet under the stairs and found them all hovering there, he gave one of his trademark scowls. 'Mother of God, can a man not have a bit of peace on his throne? It's the only place I can finish off me crossword, but that's useless now because the whole of O'Connell Street has decided to park up outside me jacks!'

But then he took his jacket from the coat stand, reached into his pocket and fanned out the circus tickets like a hand of cards, and they all grinned.

'All right, gang, let's do this!' Onion called out.

'How many times do I have to tell you?' Derek snapped back. 'I'm not in your stupid gang!'

Derek said this all the time, but Onion paid no attention to him. Of course Derek was in the gang. His membership hadn't expired merely because he'd got old and cool. Besides, it wasn't Onion's gang. He was just the reason they did things most of the time – because he was always willing to have a go at something. He kind of tried too hard at everything, but he never gave up. And most of the time he made a hash of things, but he never let it get him down. As Granny would say, 'God loves a trier', and by God did Onion try. He meant well and people considered him pretty harmless. And most of the time he was.

He'd been the first to think of the church-bell remote control. Sure, Clíona had made the gadget, but it had been Onion's idea, after he'd discovered the bell was electronic and the priest used a remote control. Derek, however, had no time for Onion's daft ideas.

'Let's do this,' Onion said again, a little quieter, and gazed up the road towards the circus lights.

Up they went to the green where the trucks were parked and the tents were pitched, as well as the van that served as the ticket office. Then they entered the Big Top. There was a big crowd, and the Five O's (well, four minus Derek) raced up the steps to grab a bench where they could all sit together with the best view of the ring. As they waited for the show to start, Granny Mary got chatting with one of the neighbours about some local scandal and the state of the world today, and Grandad Paddy went off and got candy-floss for everyone.

Onion's smile nearly split his head in half, feeling the sweet, grainy fluff melt on his tongue as the ringmaster came out, a roly-poly oul' fella with a scrunched-up face and an Elvis hairstyle, wearing a swish suit and top hat. He introduced himself as Joseph Forester, and he welcomed the audience and announced the first act.

The music started up, and the show was everything they'd hoped it would be. There were nutty clowns with a mad little car that collapsed into pieces when they stuffed too many people into it, and a spooky magician put a woman in a box and sawed it in half and then put it back together. There were dancing horses and beautiful, daring trapeze artists and the nutty clowns again and then the main event: The Great Orangini.

Even though everyone was there to see The Great Orangini, Grandad Paddy was there for the clowns. He was obsessed. 'I love the clowns – they're so funny, so talented, they're the best thing at the circus. I mean, the buckets and the confetti! There's never water in the bucket, you know? As much as I try, I always forget that there's no water in the bucket, and when the clown flings it at me from the stage, I expect to get wet, but hey presto! No water, just confetti. Genius.'

The trapeze artists set up a giant spinning wheel-shaped climbing frame, high up in the tent, and then a squat figure came bounding from behind the curtains at the back of the ring. Dressed in a baggy clown costume and heavy make-up, including a red nose and blue wig, he raised his arms, and everyone cheered as the ringmaster introduced the world-famous acrobat. He was a funny-shaped guy, with long arms and short legs, though that probably helped make him so good at what he did. Onion and the Five

CHAPTER THREE: THE GREAT ORANGINI

O's whooped and cheered as the acrobatic clown leapt up onto the spinning wheel and started doing flips, somersaults and death-defying leaps from one part of the wheel to another, all while it spun at high speed. It was dizzying for everyone to watch, but doubly so for Onion and his wonky eye, which was easily confused, especially when he was excited.

Top 5 Reasons for Onion's Eye to Go Extra Wonky

1. Lying

2. Sneezing

3. Shouting too loud

4. Seeing a girl he fancies

5. Every time he eats a ham and cheese toastie (his favourite food)

Right now, his eye was all over the place, and the acrobat looked like he was in some kind of science fiction film, flicking between different dimensions.

As the music rose, the beat got faster and then, with a scream of violins, The Great Orangini used the speed of the wheel to hurl himself somersaulting right up to the very roof of the enormous tent . . .

And then he fell.

Even the music stopped as the famous man plummeted. The shocking silence seemed to last for ever. It was as if Onion could see it all happening in slow motion. People screamed. Someone in the first row fainted. Little Molly dropped her candy-floss.

Then, when it seemed as if he must surely splat against the floor, the acrobat caught a bar at the bottom edge of the wheel and whipped back up into a somersault, landing on the top of the wheel just as it came to a stop. He struck a triumphant pose and then did a deep bow. The crowd went bananas.

'Dear God in heaven, me heart!' Granny gasped.

'That was very, very, very good – not as good as the clowns, but very good all the same!' Grandad exclaimed. 'Isn't he some fella now?'

'That was AWESOME!' Dallan shouted, jumping to his feet, his mouth gaping. 'That was totally awesome!'

'My candy-floss!' Molly cried, pointing at the floor.

Top 5 Things
Molly Cries About

1. Her reflection

2. A sad face, either on a human or a teddy

3. The theme music to the news

4. A leaf falling off a tree

5. Dogs that can't bark

All the performers came out into the ring to line up and take a bow as Orangini climbed down. Forester, the ringmaster, took the acrobat's arm and held it up in the air. As he did, Onion saw that a few centimetres of Orangini's arm showed between his glove and his sleeve. It was covered in red hair. Orangini was ginger-haired, like Onion! How cool was that?

Everyone was going nuts. But not The Great Orangini. Onion noticed that the master performer himself was not celebrating. He allowed his arm to be lifted, but as soon as he could he ducked away, walking with a shambling lope back towards the curtains. He didn't look like a man celebrating a tremendous performance. He looked like some fella who'd just finished a very ordinary job. In fact, Onion thought, he almost looked depressed.

Then he did the weirdest thing. Just before he disappeared from sight, he dropped down onto all fours, leaning on the knuckles of his hands, and pushed himself head first through the curtains.

Dallan pulled on Onion's arm.

'Do you want to try and get Orangini's autograph? He's amazing, isn't he? Fancy sneaking round the back of the tent to see if we can find him?'

'Are you joking? We could get caught, and we shouldn't be back there – it's obviously not for us. It looks so like an area where we can't go. I mean, I'd love to meet Orangini, but maybe I could send a handwritten request to the circus to see if we could make an appointment or something. What do you think?'

Dallan stared at Onion. 'You know, sometimes you're weird, just really weird,' he said as he grabbed Onion by the arm and pushed him towards the backstage entrance.

CHAPTER FOUR:
—
BORN TO BE A CLOWN

It was an overcast autumn Saturday evening, but tons of people were out from the estate. So after the show, there was a lot of standing around outside, saying how it was massive, and chatting and taking photos on phones. Grandad was still going on about the clowns. 'I think the thing that caught my eye the most was the clowns. Now, don't get me wrong, the rest of the acts were very good, but the clowns, my God – their control of confetti from a bucket is second to none.'

With all that fuss going on, nobody noticed the Five O's (minus Derek, who wasn't in their 'stupid gang') sneak off to try and find The Great Orangini.

Plastic mesh fences were up to stop people wandering into the circus's private areas, but there was a spot where the horses were kept that the kids could slip under. They came through to a smaller tent behind the Big Top where the performers waited while other acts were on. The rest of the space was taken up with the trailers, caravans and camper vans where the performers lived. Now that they'd started looking, Onion was feeling even more nervous, realising these were actually people's homes, and maybe they'd be caught.

Top 5 Things that Make Onion Nervous

1. Funny noises

2. Not having permission to do something

3. A strong breeze

4. Nettles

5. Everything, really

Curtains were closed over all the windows, so you couldn't see in from the outside.

'Ah, come on, let's get out of here,' Sive said, chewing her gum and looking bored, which was how she dealt with being nervous. Actually, it was how she dealt with everything. 'This is stupid. What are we gonna do, start knocking on all the doors?'

'Well . . . couldn't we just knock on all the doors?' Clíona asked.

They all thought Clíona was probably a genius, but not at everything. When it came to dealing with people, she was a bit dim.

'No,' Sive said firmly. 'We are not going to do that.'

But Onion was half-ready to do exactly that. He couldn't stop thinking about Orangini dropping onto all fours as he left the ring and how odd it had looked. Onion fiddled with the inhaler hanging round his neck, which he tended to do when he was thinking of doing something daft.

He'd get Dallan to do the talking. Dallan believed himself to be more grown up than the rest of them, but he was good at talking.

Orangini was the headline star in the circus, so Onion figured he would have the nicest home. Either him or the ringmaster. Only one trailer was obviously fancier than the others – cream coloured, larger and newer looking, with big windows at one end. Walking to that end, Onion stood on tiptoes to see if he could get a view inside.

'Onion, knock it off!' Sive called. 'That's so nosy!'

But then, as if she'd decided he'd now broken through the nosy wall, she came up beside him and put her fingers on the window ledge. The curtains were open, so when they lifted their heads they were able to see inside.

In a moment of shock, they both yanked their heads right down again and turned to the others, their eyes wide.

CHAPTER FOUR: BORN TO BE A CLOWN

'What is it?' Clíona whispered.

'The Ferg's in there with the ringmaster!' Onion gasped, just a little too loud.

Dallan shoved a hand over his friend's mouth to keep him quiet and took a quick peek for himself. 'He could be here for us!' he said in a hoarse whisper. 'It's a trap! The guards are running a sting operation to nail us for the church bell job!'

'The "church bell job"?' Clíona whimpered, turning unusually white.

'"A sting operation"?' Sive snorted quietly, rolling her eyes. 'Gimme a break.'

'He's not here for us,' Onion said uncertainly. 'Is he? Do you really think he's here for us?'

'Quiet, you eejits! He doesn't even know who we are,' Sive hissed at them. 'Everybody shush – let's try and listen.'

And so they did. The trailer had thin walls and the men inside were speaking in bombastic voices, so it wasn't hard.

'You've done well for yourself, Joe, I'll give you that,' The Ferg was saying. 'All those years ago when we were in clown school together, I thought I was pretty good, but you were on another level. The shape of your red nose, the craftsmanship that went into those squeaky shoes, the long pointy chin—'

'That was my real chin,' answered Forester.

'And what a chin! No doubt about it, you were born to be a clown.'

'Nice of you to say so, Fergus,' the ringmaster replied.

'And look at you now, with your own circus. Impressive, very impressive.'

'I like to think I've built up a nice little operation,' Forester said. 'You've got to gather the right people around you.'

'Well, you've certainly found the goose that laid the golden egg – The Great Orangini!' The admiration was clear from The Ferg's voice. 'What a performer, Joe! What a discovery! I've never seen anything like him. I think he could be even better than you were in your prime!'

'Well, you know the acrobatics were always just a sideline for me,' Forester grunted, sounding slightly less than happy with the comparison. 'Humour was my true calling. But how have you been? Police work, eh? A guardian of the peace, no less! It must be an exciting life.'

'Right you are there,' The Ferg said, then added modestly, 'as it happens, I took down a dangerous gang of young criminals today, single-handed, before they could rob the church. Pretty major operation, if I say so myself.'

'What a load of rubbish! We were never going to rob the church!' Dallan muttered, almost loud enough for the two men to hear. Onion gave him a thump on the arm to shut him up.

'Still, though, I often think back to those years in clown school,' The Ferg went on. 'I mean, don't get me wrong, I love being a guard, but I always felt I had it in me to be a clown. Even now, people laugh at me all the time.'

'Do they really?' Forester asked.

'Oh yes. I suppose you can't help it when clowning's in your blood. My fellow guards, now, they'd often tell me I'm a clown. They can see my gift for humour.'

'I'd well believe it, Fergus.'

'My partner, Bridie, she says it to me all the time. "Fergus Plunkett," she says, "you're a right clown."'

'She has a good eye, that one, I can tell,' Forester said.

'So . . .' The Ferg's seat squeaked as he shifted nervously in it. 'I don't suppose . . . I mean, it would be a huge honour, if . . .'

'You could meet The Great Orangini?' Forester finished for him.

'Do you think I could?'

'No,' the ringmaster replied. 'You have to understand, even for a fine man of your standing, Fergus, for one of life's natural clowns, I can't make an exception. He's a shooting star in front of an audience, but take off the make-up and he's such a quiet, private man.'

'I suppose so many of the great ones are, eh?' The Ferg said knowingly.

'You said it.' Forester sighed. 'Now, if you'll excuse me, I'm afraid I have to see to preparations for the late show.'

'Of course, of course!' Garda Plunkett said, though the disappointment in his voice was obvious. 'Perhaps we could get together for another drink before you leave town?'

'I'm always happy to see a former classmate,' Forester told him. 'Why don't I call you after the final show, and we can have a proper chat about old times?'

The four kids hadn't noticed, but Forester was already on his feet and now he opened the door on the side, near their end of the trailer. They pressed themselves against the end wall as the two men descended the steps. Dallan was pointing frantically at something. The gate in the fence was a few metres from where they were standing. The Ferg was going to walk right past them. He was bound to see them.

Another trailer was parked behind Forester's. Fire-engine red, with a woman trapeze artist painted on the side, it was a smaller, older, more battered version of the ringmaster's. With seconds to spare, Sive dived underneath it, and the others quickly followed. They watched The Ferg's uniformed legs walk past and on out the gate in the temporary fence. Moments later,

CHAPTER FOUR: BORN TO BE A CLOWN

Forester strode over to the gate to watch the guard go, a strange expression on his face as he stared after his old classmate.

Then he turned around and glared at the trailer where the Five O's were hiding, a bitter scowl on his face.

CHAPTER FIVE:
ORANGINI UNMASKED

The four kids dragged themselves in behind the set of steel steps that led up to the door on the end of the red trailer, cowering as far out of sight underneath as they could get.

Forester had his hat off, revealing his Elvis hairstyle, and seemed a lot less glamorous in the dull grey light of an Irish evening. He looked in a rotten mood too, his sharp nose sticking out of his round, grimacing face like a giant tooth. He hurried over to the very trailer the kids were hiding under. He raced up the steps, opened the door and a small mass of hair fell out onto his foot. It was the Great Orangini's blue wig.

CHAPTER FIVE: ORANGINI UNMASKED

Onion's wonky eye went wild. This must be Orangini's trailer!

Cursing to himself, Forester kicked the wig back inside. 'How many times do I have to tell you to keep this place tidy!' he bellowed. 'Girl, you are in serious trouble. I saw what you did out in the ring, Maya. You never, never use your hands to walk when you're out in public. Have you got that? If people find out what's going on here, we're finished. **FINISHED!** Is that what you want? Is it?'

Then he stepped into the trailer and slammed the door behind him. The latch didn't click closed properly, and the door swung back open just a few centimetres. Barely enough for someone to put their eye to the crack and peer inside.

The Five O's looked at each other, curiosity burning through their brains.

'Oh God, why are we here, why are we doing this? I know, I know, it's because we want to. But we shouldn't be here! But let's stay until we have to go. But I'd love to go now.' Onion was getting nervous.

Like four small Irish ninjas, they slipped out from under the trailer and arranged themselves by height, Onion, Clíona, Sive and Dallan, so they could all get an eye to the crack in the door.

Inside, they saw the strangest scene. One of the trapeze artists, a guy with a head the shape of a bucket, was sitting in a chair holding a monkey. No, not a monkey, Onion corrected himself – a young ape. An orang-utan. The creature had two tufts of ginger hair done up in blue bows and was wearing a pink ballet costume.

However, that wasn't even the weirdest thing. Sitting at the far end of the trailer, dressed in Orangini's outfit, except for the wig, nose and make-up, was an adult orang-utan. The rear section of the trailer was taken up with a cage, which had two bunks and some climbing bars built into it. Scattered around the floor were pet toys and bits of fruit and vegetables. So where was The Great Orangini?

CHAPTER FIVE: ORANGINI UNMASKED

'Róisín, get this mess tidied up,' Forester snapped.

The young ape gave a frightened yelp and immediately jumped out of the trapeze artist's lap and started cleaning up. She put the bits of food in a bin in the corner and bounded around placing the toys in cupboards and on shelves. Once the place was looking tidy, she scampered over to the adult ape and cuddled into her arms. The adult, who was obviously her mother, stroked her ears gently.

But Forester wasn't done with his complaining. 'The Great Orangini is supposed to be a HUMAN!' he snarled at the mother ape. He made some kind of gesture with his hands. 'Do you understand that, you silly sow? You do not walk around on your blinkin' hands! And stop looking so depressed when you're out there. You're spoiling the mood. You're a star, Maya! Or, at least, you're pretending to be a star. Try and act the part, for pity's sake.'

Onion couldn't believe what he was hearing. The Great Orangini was an ape? That explained the incredible acrobatics he – she – could do. And no wonder nobody had ever seen 'him' without his make-up. This was crazy stuff. Forester turned to the guy whose head was shaped like a bucket – which, as it turned out, was also his name.

'Bucket, you have to stop fussing over Róisín,' Forester went on. 'She's supposed to stay in the cage until the audience has left the area. Go get Truck. We're putting the chains back on Maya.'

CHAPTER FIVE: ORANGINI UNMASKED

Bucket looked like he wanted to protest, but he didn't speak. Instead, he turned to Róisín and made some motions with his hands, looking like he was worried about her. The Five O's recognised this: sign language. Sive's family used it because her father was deaf. Sive had impaired hearing too and wore a hearing aid. Maybe Róisín knew it, too. Clíona had told them all about a chimpanzee that learned sign language so that it could communicate with humans, but as usual they only half listened to what she was saying.

Forester watched Bucket for a second and then replied, 'Stop talking to Róisín and do as I say! If she's not going to do as she's told, she gets punished. Why do you insist on staying silent all the time? It's so infuriating! Now, take Róisín off her and – oh, never mind, I'll get Truck to do it.'

The four kids got a fright, ducking away from the door as the ringmaster came towards them. They scrambled back under the trailer in a mad rush as he swung the door open and roared out:

'TRUCK! GET YOUR BACKSIDE IN HERE!
AND BRING THE CHAINS!'

The gang watched as a woman stepped out of the next caravan over. She was the largest, most muscular woman any of them had ever seen. Onion remembered her from the clown-car bit of the show, but she didn't look funny now, dressed in a vest top, her clown trousers and some Doc Martens. She must have been about two metres tall and it would be fair to say she was built like a truck, which was probably where she got her name. Her long black hair hung in thick locks over her back and shoulders. She was carrying a heavy set of chains in her huge hands. The four kids shuddered as they felt the thuds of her feet through the ground. She walked up to the steps, right in front of them, and climbed into the trailer over their heads. It creaked under her weight.

'Hey there, Bucket, my love,' they heard the woman say in a heavy Belfast accent. 'Great show tonight. Right then – Maya been a bad girl, has she? Back in the chains you go, yeh wee ginger-nut.'

It was a voice that expected to be obeyed. There came the sound of movement and the clink of the chains and then manacles being snapped into place. Onion bit his lip and crept out from under the trailer. He had to see what was going on. The door had failed to latch properly again, though it was almost completely closed. Sive was shaking her head frantically at him. Onion reached up, got his fingernails to the edge of the door and pulled it open just the slightest crack.

'Bucket,' he heard Forester say. 'Keep the little one away from that door. She won't leave her mother, but there's no point giving her ideas. And make sure you get that latch fixed tonight.'

Onion decided that these were exceptional circumstances. He would use his good eye, just this once. He raised his head up to the level of the floor, squeezed his right eye shut and lifted his glasses to move the patch away from his good left eye, as if it gave him some kind of super-vision. He pressed it to the crack in the door . . .

And he found himself looking right into someone else's eye.

Róisín, the young ape, had crept up to the door and had her head down there, right in front of him. His breath caught in his throat, which was the only thing that stopped him from screaming in fright. She screeched, though, loud enough for both of them. She leapt to her feet and, in doing so, knocked the door wide open. The young orang-utan stood there, staring out at him.

CHAPTER FIVE: ORANGINI UNMASKED

Onion dived back under the trailer before anyone else could see him, but Róisín was gazing into the open space in front of her. It was as if this mysterious red-headed boy she'd seen was a bolt of inspiration. There was no obstacle in front of her, no one to stand between her and freedom.

With one leap, the young orang-utan in the ballet costume flew out of the trailer, landed on the grass and darted away through the trailers and camper vans. In seconds, she'd vanished. There came a wail from her mother, inside the trailer, the clatter of chains and then the hard sounds of feet running towards the door and down the steps. Bucket hurtled out, racing after the little ape, then Truck thumped down, heading after them, though not as fast.

And finally, Forester hopped down, more agile than you'd expect of a man his shape. He didn't run after the others. His legs stayed there, visible just beyond the steps. He was sure he'd heard something when Róisín was escaping, a sound from underneath. He turned around, bent down and peered under the trailer.

But when he stared through the steps into the space underneath, there was nothing to be seen. Whoever had been there was gone.

CHAPTER SIX:
—
THE USE OF WILD ANIMALS

The four Five O's legged it back to Onion's house, avoiding the crowd that lingered around the circus tents. When they got up to his and Derek's bedroom, it was clear that everyone was utterly freaked out. This whole thing was all sorts of wrong, but they didn't know what to do about it. Apart from having a go at Onion, of course.

'What the—? I mean, what—? Like, why? Whyyy?!' Sive exclaimed, her hands on her cheeks. For once, she'd forgotten to top up her chewing gum and her mouth was free to shout. 'Are. You. Mad?

WHY DID YOU OPEN THE DOOR?'
She finally got it out of her angry mouth.

'I just wanted to see what was going on,' Onion said helplessly.

'We ALL wanted to see what was going on!' Dallan snapped at him.

'And by God did we all get to see what was going on!' said Sive, 'But that doesn't mean you should have opened the door, Onion. Why did you open the door?'

'Because I was STUPID! Okay?' Onion cried. 'Are you happy now?'

'Why would we be happy now?' Sive asked in a shrill voice. 'Because of us, a circus has lost their orang-utan and it's running wild in Ballinlud, and I'm pretty sure you're not supposed to pretend an ape is a human acrobat, but ... but ... maybe that's normal in circuses? And then they're being really nasty to her and keeping her in chains and –'

'That's illegal,' Clíona said firmly. 'Keeping an orang-utan in a circus. It's illegal.'

CHAPTER SIX: THE USE OF WILD ANIMALS

'What makes you so sure?' Sive asked.

'Oh, here we go,' said Dallan.

'Because it's a law,' Clíona replied, giving them all a 'duh' look. 'The Circuses (Prohibition on Use of Wild Animals) Regulations 2017. It's, like, totally illegal to use wild animals in a circus in Ireland.'

'How do you know this stuff?' Dallan asked.

'How do you *not* know this stuff?' she retorted.

Clíona took her phone from her pocket. She was the only one of the four who had a phone, which would have been useful if she wasn't always trying to make something else out of it. This meant that she almost never had a phone, just a half-finished invention that rarely worked. It looked like this was one of those rare occasions when the phone was actually a working phone.

'We have to call the guards,' she said.

'Whoa, whoa, whoa!' Dallan grabbed the phone from her. 'You're not calling anyone!'

'Why not?'

'You were there! You heard Forester talking to The Ferg! They've been mates for years,' Dallan said fearfully. 'Who do you think will show up here if the guards are called in? And if The Ferg gets called in, he'll find out who we are. He'll know where we live. He'll tell our parents we were messing around at the school. And then they'll know we were poking around at the circus too. We'll be grounded for ever. We need to keep a low profile and let all this madness cool down.'

'We could just phone them and tell them about the orang-utans and not give our names?' Onion suggested.

'They can trace the call,' Dallan insisted. 'The minute you switch that thing on, you may as well have a beacon on your head – or, worse still, a very tall man on your head shouting and pointing. They know, they aaaaalways knowww.'

Dallan had a very lively imagination.

'He's right, guys. The phone companies even have software that sends information to the police station to tell the guards where you are, what you are, who you are ...' explained Onion to a very confused-looking gang.

'I don't think they'll be, like, tracing calls or – or sending the guards after us.' Clíona shook her head. 'That doesn't sound like a proportional response.'

'A what?' Onion asked.

'Hang on, hang on, we don't have to do anything,' Sive reassured them, holding her hands out to try and calm things down. 'Right now, there's an orang-utan in a ballet dress running around Ballinlud. That's the kind of thing people tend to notice – you don't get much of it in Dublin. Someone will see her, figure out she's from the circus and call the guards or the ISPCA or something. It'll all be taken care of. We don't have to do anything. It's as good as sorted.'

There was a bit more grumbling and protesting, but keeping quiet and doing nothing sounded like a pretty good idea because it was easy, and nobody had a better one. In the end, they all agreed it had been a freaky day and they should try and make Sunday a bit more chilled and maybe stay out of trouble for a while. They shook hands on it, and then Sive, Dallan and Clíona headed home.

Onion said his goodbyes and closed the front door, then turned to find Derek standing right behind him, tapping away on his phone. He was a head taller than his younger brother, and he was everything Onion wasn't: handsome, muscular, popular, good at sports and incredibly suspicious of everyone. He also saw it as his job to make Onion's life a nightmare.

Top 5 Ways Derek Has Made Onion's Life a Nightmare

1. Giving him a dead arm every time he passes

2. Breathing into his face with his stinky teenager breath

3. Farting into his hand and then shoving it in Onion's face

CHAPTER SIX: THE USE OF WILD ANIMALS

4. Ignoring him all day

5. Always claiming he's not in Onion's 'stupid gang'

'So, what was all the shouting about?' Derek asked, without looking up from the screen.

'Nothing,' Onion said automatically.

'Yeah, right. Look, Granny and Grandad have gone down the pub,' Derek told him. He lifted his head to stare at his little brother. 'Come on, something's up. I heard you talking about the guards. What was it? You didn't kidnap Mr Kerrigan's cat again, did you?'

'We never kidnapped her,' Onion retorted. 'That's not fair. She chased a rat into Dallan's bag and then fell asleep in there after she ate the thing.'

'Yiz took her to the National Gallery,' Derek reminded him.

'No, she went with us to the National Gallery,' Onion objected. 'It's not the same thing at all. It was a school tour and that cat was just resting in the bag. Okay, so she got out, but we caught her eventually. It was a load of fuss over nothing . . .'

'Tell that to the nice lady who had a raging cat climb onto her head and get tangled in her hair.' Derek made a sorrowful face. 'Onion, she had the hair ripped off her.'

'That was – That was ages ago! Why'd you have to keep bringing that up?'

'Because I want to, ya sap,' said Derek, as he gave Onion a dead arm.

'Owwwww!' cried Onion. 'Anyway, we're not up to nothing now!'

'So you're telling me absolutely nothing happened after the circus?' Derek asked, staring into his little brother's wonky eye.

Onion silently cursed his eye as he squeezed it shut, trying to hide the fact that it was turning in. It was like having a lie detector in your eye socket.

'Yeeeaaah, yiz are up to something, all right.' Derek cackled, nodding to himself as he turned around and walked towards the kitchen. 'Don't worry, I'll find out. You'll break eventually, Onion. You always do. And then you'll tell me everything.'

'Leave me alone!' Onion shouted after him. 'The Five O's are supposed to look after each other! Why are you never on my side?'

'Because I'm not in your stupid gang!'

CHAPTER SEVEN:
—
SOMETHING IN THE NIGHT

O nion couldn't sleep. His nerves were crackling, stressed with thoughts of getting caught by the guards and what he'd seen at the circus and the argument with his mates. Rubbing his bleary eyes, he put his glasses on, got up and went downstairs to get a drink of water. He didn't bother turning on the lights. He filled the glass at the kitchen sink and started drinking it right there, gazing out into the darkness of the back garden.

Something moved out there, near the hedge at the back. Onion nearly choked on the water. Setting the glass down on the counter, he coughed and looked hard into the gloom. An intruder was out there, staring at the house. The figure crept along the side wall, coming closer. And as it did, Onion felt the breath freeze in his chest. Instinctively, he reached for his inhaler, which normally hung around his neck. Not now, however. It was still upstairs on the locker beside his bed. That immediately made his breathing worse. He kept staring out the window.

It wasn't a robber, it was . . . a ghost of some kind. It couldn't be a normal human. It was wearing a pale flouncy dress, like a little girl, but it was strangely misshapen. It looked more like a beast of some kind, perhaps a weird undead creature or . . . or . . .

No. It was an orang-utan.

His breathing eased up. There was no doubt about it: it was Róisín, from the circus, in her pink ballet costume. Onion gaped in amazement and went to open the utility room door, and then stopped. He might frighten her off. She was probably really scared to be out in the dark on her own. Maybe it was the first time she'd ever been away from the circus. He reached over to the fruit bowl on the counter and picked up a banana. Then he moved quietly towards the utility room.

Opening the back door as gently as he could, he waved the banana at Róisín. She was huddled by the pole of the rotary clothesline, which didn't even hide her a little bit, but maybe it made her feel safer. He waved the banana again and, ever so slowly, she came forward, walking on all fours using the knuckles of her hands. Her arms were very long and her legs were short, so she hardly had to bend forward at all to do this.

Stopping a couple of paces away from him, she leaned in, reaching shyly for the banana. Onion went to hold it out and in a flash she'd grabbed it and dashed back to the far end of the garden. Forget peeling it – he watched her bite right through the skin and wolf down the flesh. But then she started creeping back. Onion went and got an apple this time. He put it on the ground just outside the door and moved back. Róisín came much closer this time, picked up the apple and only moved back as far as the clothesline. She grinned widely, showing him her big teeth, and gobbled the apple.

She put fingertips to her chin and pushed them forward. Onion had seen Sive do this loads of times. Róisín was like her mother – she knew sign language. That movement was the sign for 'Thank you'. He made the rolling hands motion for 'You're welcome'. He knew about five things in sign, so this wasn't going to be much of a conversation. He needed Sive here, but he couldn't call her house in the middle of the night.

It wasn't right to leave a young ape from . . . the Amazon, or the Congo, or ... Where were orang-utans from? He'd have to look it up. Anyway, he couldn't leave her wandering outside at night in a Ballinlud housing estate. There was nothing else for it, he decided. Róisín would have to sleep in the house. If he could get her to be quiet, he could sneak her upstairs and hide her in the attic.

After a couple more bananas and a nectarine, Róisín seemed to trust him. He got her to follow him inside, took some more fruit from the bowl and a big cup of water and they crept into the dark hallway. Róisín gazed around, eyes wide, taking in this strange place. Onion guessed she'd never been in a normal house before, having lived her whole life hidden away in circus trailers. He wondered how old she was. She was a good bit smaller than him, but he had no idea how it worked with apes.

CHAPTER SEVEN: SOMETHING IN THE NIGHT

He realised he was climbing the stairs on his own. Róisín had stopped to examine Derek's phone, which was charging in the hall. He wasn't allowed to have it in their room at night. Róisín went to put it in her mouth and Onion nearly screamed. The thought of what Derek would do if an orang-utan ate his phone . . . Forcing himself to stay calm, Onion gave her a big friendly smile and gently tugged the phone out of her hands and put it back on the hall table.

Then she jumped into the clothes basket and popped back up with all the clothes on her head. Onion pulled them off her, but then she grabbed Grandad's ceramic clown off the shelf. Onion grabbed that and put it back, but as he replaced it, Róisín just grabbed another one and another one. She was too fast! Onion tried his best to keep Róisín quiet until she eventually found a small ceramic lady dressed in Spanish clothes with a bell under her dress. Oh no! Just as Róisín was about to ring the tiny bell, Onion managed to snatch it from her hands and replace it on the shelf. His grandparents would never know a thing.

Róisín, having had enough of the tiny ceramic people, scampered past him, making him bump into the coat stand and knock it over. It didn't make much noise because it was mostly soft stuff, but the jackets and coats went everywhere. Shaking his head, he told himself he'd come back down and clear up after he'd got her into the attic.

He'd barely got a few steps up the stairs, sneaking ever so carefully over the squeaky

steps, thinking Róisín was down by his feet, when a shadow suddenly loomed over him and he nearly shrieked again. She'd leapt up onto the banister and scooted easily up to the landing on hands and feet without even touching the stairs. Onion wished he could do that; those squeaky steps were a real pain. He took a long breath to ease his shaky nerves, clutched the fruit and cup to his chest, splashing water on his T-shirt, then hurried after her.

Now for the really tricky part. He got the pole for the attic hatch and reached up with it. He was just about tall enough to reach the brass loop with the hook, then he slowly, slowly pulled the hatch down. The spring-loaded hinges squeaked loudly, as they always did, and Róisín cowered away. Onion froze, waiting for someone to call out or come out of their room . . . Nothing. With the hatch down, he unfolded the wooden ladder and, holding the supplies with one hand and using the other to climb, made his way up to the attic.

It was gloomy and dusty, but at least there was a light he could leave on so Róisín wouldn't be left in the dark. The place was packed with boxes and tied-up bags and all the other junk that got dumped in a family's attic over the years. Though it might not be ideal, she'd be safe there until the morning, when he could get the Five O's together and they could figure out what they were going to do.

He was heading down the ladder again, leaving the fruit and water with Róisín, when she went to follow him. He held up his hand, motioning to the attic space.

'No,' he whispered. 'You have to stay here. It's not safe to come down. We have to make sure nobody sees you.'

Either she didn't understand or she didn't want to. She let out a cry that was part begging and part fear. She made a gesture that he assumed meant 'Don't leave me alone'.

'Ssshhh! I have to go. Ssshhh! Please don't. Don't make any noise,' he begged her.

CHAPTER SEVEN: SOMETHING IN THE NIGHT

He gazed at her helplessly, seeing how upset she was becoming. Looking down onto the landing and then back at the ape in his attic, he sighed and nodded, and then climbed back up.

'Okay, I'll stay for a while, but just a few minutes, okay?'

So he sat with his back against a box and she crawled into his lap and he stroked her ears like he'd seen her mother do.

And soon, they both fell fast asleep.

CHAPTER EIGHT:
—
DESPERATE MEASURES

O nion woke in stages of fright that increased in intensity as his brain slowly came online. He was uncomfortable. Why? Because he was slumped on bare, dusty plywood with his head against a cardboard box. Why? A few seconds of thinking . . . Last night. The orang-utan. That was mad. Creeping upstairs. What time was it? He didn't know. So if he was up here, where was the orang-utan? Where was Róisín?

He sat bolt upright. The hatch was still open. The hatch was open! Holy Bono! . . . WHERE WAS Róisín?

CHAPTER EIGHT: DESPERATE MEASURES

Just when he was sure his heart was going to stop dead, he looked around and saw her hanging from one of the rafters at the other end of the attic. She gave him a little wave and he put a hand to his chest and nearly fainted with relief. Scanning the place, he thought everything looked okay. In fact, he could have sworn that the attic seemed tidier than it had been last night. Still, though, his problems were only starting. What was he going to do now?

Luckily, he must have woken early because he was so uncomfortable. Nobody else was up yet. Onion did his best to get Róisín to understand she needed to stay quiet, then he made his way down the ladder and, as silently as he could, closed the attic hatch. He hurried back to the room he shared with Derek and checked his clock: half seven. Granny would be up soon, and so would Molly, who didn't understand the idea of lie-ins at weekends. Grandad would sleep later. Derek was in his bed, snoring softly, and would sleep as long as he could before Granny took the kids to half-ten Mass. Whatever Onion was going to do, he'd have to do it soon.

If he used the house phone to call his friends' houses, their parents would want to know why he was calling so early. He shook his head, all wound up with stress and frustration. This was a serious situation. What was he going to do?

His gaze fell on a black rectangular box about the size of a remote control that lay on his small desk. Clíona had left her invention behind. His eyes narrowed and, looking out, he could see the church steeple in the distance, over the roofs of the estate. This was a serious situation. He had an ape hidden in his attic. Desperate measures were called for.

Picking up the remote, he pressed the button.

Out in the chilly morning air, the church bell rang . . . way, way too early. All across the Dublin suburb of Ballinlud, heads were messed with as people woke in a panic thinking they'd slept in and missed Mass. Father Murphy came running out of his house in his pyjamas, remote control for the bell in his hand, pointing it frantically at the church. It stopped, but as he walked back into his house it started ringing again! What was going on? He ran back out, pointed the remote at the bell, pressed the button and it stopped ringing. He waited a second to make sure it had worked then walked calmly back inside the house . . . only to hear the bell ringing again! This time Father Murphy ran out, threw the remote in the direction of the bell and went back inside his house once more, slamming the door behind him. He was so angry he'd have to go to confession.

But a few streets down, as if summoned by the Bat Signal, the three Five O's came running.

CHAPTER NINE:

—

ONION EXPLAINS THE PLAN

Onion stood by the front door, waiting for the others to arrive. He noticed the coat stand was empty of coats, and it took him a few seconds to remember that he'd knocked it over during the night. He must have stood it up and forgotten about it. But where were the coats? Eyes narrowing, he tried to remember where he had put them and why he hadn't just hung them back on the hooks. Not wanting to be caught here if Granny came down the stairs and started asking questions, he went out into the front garden.

A drone flew past overhead. Onion had never owned one himself, though Clíona had one she played with sometimes – when she wasn't busy taking it apart or putting it back together. This one looked serious, flying high and steady, and pretty fast too. It was sweeping in wide circles, as if it was searching for something in particular. He wondered what it could be.

The thought was interrupted by the arrival of his friends, one after another. Sive, Dallan and Clíona all looked ready to tear strips off him. He was able to keep them quiet enough to sneak upstairs to his room, but he couldn't take them into the attic. Each one was as annoyed as the next:

'This better be good – I was having a lovely sleep. I need my beauty sleep, you know, Onion,' said Dallan.

'I can't believe I'm here. I was relaxing with a nice book about the Russian Front in World War Two,' said Clíona.

'I simply hate you, Onion,' moaned Sive.

Granny would be getting up any minute now and there was no way to get in and out of that squeaky hatch before she did. The only reason she hadn't lifted out of the bed like a racehorse at the starting gate was probably because she hadn't heard the bell over Grandad's snoring. Luckily Derek was in the bathroom, admiring his reflection in the mirror as usual, so they could talk in his room without Derek giving Onion a dead arm for bringing an ape into the house.

It took about a minute to explain about the orang-utan, and then another five minutes to convince them that he wasn't taking the mickey.

CHAPTER NINE: ONION EXPLAINS THE PLAN

Clíona was sitting on the bed, rocking back and forth with her hands over her ears. Dallan thought it was the coolest thing he'd ever heard, but they were probably all going to prison. Sive was chewing gum and trying to fake boredom because she was obviously in a state of shock.

'We can't send her back,' Onion reasoned with them. 'Forester and those others, they were being really mean to her mother. And with Forester and The Ferg being old mates, we can't call in the guards. So we have to do something ourselves. We have to take action.'

They all turned to stare at him.

'Are you saying what I think you're saying?' Dallan asked.

'I'm saying we have to break her mother out of the circus,' Onion said firmly. 'We can't keep Róisín and leave Maya there with those people.'

'Keep Róisín?' Sive repeated.

'Yes. We're going to keep them both here. They can live with us.'

'Live with us in Ballinlud?' Clíona perked up, suddenly intrigued. 'How?'

'I don't know. Somehow.' Onion gulped. 'I haven't worked that bit out yet.'

'What have you worked out?' Sive inquired.

'Okay, well . . . none of it really. But that's why I called you lot.'

When you're as blindly optimistic as Onion, everything seems possible, and his optimism was contagious. And right there, in that moment, he was offering them a dream that seized their imaginations. The dream that they could be friends with two orang-utans, helping them to live a secret existence in the suburb of Ballinlud. Real live apes that could perhaps become local legends, like Big Foot or the Abominable Snowman. That would be totally cool.

'It would be like having our own Wookiee!' Dallan exclaimed.

'That's a bit insulting, don't you think?' Sive said.

'To Wookiees or orang-utans?' Onion asked.

'You can't compare them. Wookiees are an ancient, civilised race,' Clíona said. Then, attempting to be realistic, 'But you still can't keep an orang-utan as a pet.'

'They wouldn't be pets, they'd be friends,' Onion pointed out. 'That's different. We wouldn't own them. They could live in the wild. They belong in the wild.'

'In the wild. In . . . Ballinlud?' Sive stared at him, wanting to be convinced.

They all turned to gaze out the window at the street of identical semi-detached houses, surrounded by many more streets of very similar semi-detached houses.

'A man in a film had an orang-utan as a pet. Or a friend, I think,' Dallan said helpfully. 'Though it was an old film. And it was America.'

'Loads of people have apes as pets in America,' Onion said, though he wasn't that sure about it. He thought you could say just about anything about America and it would be true. 'Anyway, first things first. We have to break Maya out of the circus. Then we can figure out where's the best place for them to live.'

'And before that, you have to go to Mass,' Sive told him. 'From the sounds of it, your granny's out of bed.'

'Someone's going to have to stay here with Róisín,' Onion told them. 'Grandad doesn't do Mass. If she makes a noise while we're gone, he'll find her for sure.'

It would have made sense for Sive to stay with the ape, as she was the one who was fluent in sign language, but her family went to Mass every Sunday too. Dallan's and Clíona's families didn't, so the duty to mind Róisín fell to them. Onion told them he'd distract his grandparents so Dallan and Clíona could sneak into the attic and stay there ape-sitting until Onion got back. Sive would keep watch for Derek and Molly while they went up through the hatch.

CHAPTER NINE: ONION EXPLAINS THE PLAN

There was a slight chance that Derek might get sick of his own reflection and catch them. Molly would come straight downstairs when she woke up, eager for breakfast. They had to work this just right.

It went wrong, almost from the start. Derek stumbled out of the bathroom, half-asleep, even as Onion was starting down the stairs. He pushed past Onion, stumbling on down the steps, as if he had somewhere to be.

'Hey, where's my phone?' he called out when he reached the hall table.

Onion clutched his inhaler and walked past as if he hadn't heard the question, but he felt the sudden urge to pee. Derek's phone. Róisín had picked it up and tried to eat it last night. Onion had fallen asleep and left the hatch open. The ape could have been down here for hours.

Granny, Grandad and Molly were all downstairs. Grandad had his paper open at the kitchen table.

'If this government continues to govern we won't have a government to govern us,' said Grandad as Granny rolled her eyes.

Molly was dressed in her mismatched garb and her hair was tied up in bunches. She was holding a whisk and was using it to try to turn her Weetabix into marshmallows.

'Abra-cab-leaba, turn my 'eetabix into marshmallows,' she said as she waved her magic whisk, but nothing happened.

Granny was at the sink trying to get a stain out of a bigger stain on the table cloth. 'I swear to God, these stains in stains are a nightmare. Oh, morning, love,' she said to Onion. 'You don't know what happened to all the fruit, do you?'

Oh, batterballs. The fruit.

'I ate it. I was a bit hungry last night,' Onion said without thinking, then winced at his own stupidity.

CHAPTER NINE: ONION EXPLAINS THE PLAN

'You ate fruit?' Granny exclaimed. 'You ate all that fruit? Do you hear this, Paddy, what Onion's saying? He ate fruit.'

'I can see the headlines now,' Grandad grunted from behind the paper, stretching his hand out in the air above it, '"Miracle in Ballinlud".'

'I eat apples sometimes!' Onion protested.

'When I put them in your lunchbox!' Granny chuckled as she reached for the dishwasher. 'You do be starving at school. But bananas? Nectarines? Ah, but I shouldn't laugh. That's great if you're eating fruit now, love. You've turned over a new leaf. You might even be eating leaves next. Salads an' all that. I'm proud of you. I tell you, though, we're going to need a bigger bowl.'

Onion could have sighed with relief. That had gone okay. Then Granny opened the dishwasher. Folded up on the two racks were all the coats that should have been hanging on the coat stand. Molly pointed and burst into a fit of giggles.

'What in heaven's name is all this?' Granny gasped.

'Where's my phone?' Derek demanded, storming into the kitchen. 'Get your stupid

friends out of my room, Onion! This place is starting to smell like a crèche.'

'I don't know anything about your stupid phone!' Onion snapped at his big brother. 'You've probably lost it again, like you're always doing.'

'Why are all the coats in the dishwasher?' Granny asked in a bewildered voice.

'I'll put every one of yiz in the dishwasher if you don't quiet down and let me read me paper!' Grandad roared.

'If you don't tell me where my phone is, you're a dead man!' Derek growled at Onion.

'Derek, I'll not have threats like that in this house!' Granny warned.

Onion tried not to let his wonky eye jerk upwards as he heard the faint squeak of the attic hatch opening upstairs. He took a blast of his inhaler, then looked from his brother to his sister to his granny and then to his grandad. Taking a deep breath, he tried to come up with some kind of explanation for what was going on, but all that came out was: 'I think we all need to go to Mass!'

CHAPTER TEN:
—
NOT YOUR TYPICAL SUNDAY MORNING

T hanks to his grandparents' lack of attention to the children in their care, Onion managed to get his family, minus Grandad, out of the house without them wondering where two of his friends had disappeared to. He and Sive agreed to meet up immediately after Mass. It was a long service, the priest talking about being kind to all God's creatures, especially cats. He had a lot of stories about his cats. While Granny hung around with Molly afterwards to catch up on the latest goings-on with the neighbours, Derek met some of his mates to chat up a bunch of girls in real life, since he had no phone to contact them with.

Onion and Sive hurried back to his house. Their minds were all a-flurry with thoughts about what to do with the orang-utan in the attic and how to break her mother out of the circus.

It wasn't your typical Sunday morning.

When they got in, Grandad Paddy was lying on the kitchen floor with his toolbox beside him, his head stuck into the cupboard under the sink where he was fixing something. Grandad was old enough to retire, but he probably never would. He was a handyman who fixed whatever needed fixing in the local area, although when he fixed something, it usually broke more, and it tended to take a long time and many cups of tea. He wasn't very good at his job but at least he was always in business.

Top 5 Things that Grandad Fixed but Actually Made Worse

1. The back door was getting stuck so he took it off, shaved it down, put it back on and now there's a massive gap at the bottom where the wind howls in.

2. The toilet wouldn't flush properly, so Grandad had a go and now it takes four push-downs to make it flush.

3. The head on the mop was a bit loose so Grandad fixed it. Now every time Granny tries to mop the floor, the head falls off into the bucket.

4. The toaster only toasts bread on one side after Grandad fixed it because he thought his toast wasn't toasty enough.

5. He fixed the leaky hot tap, but now the hot water comes out of the cold tap.

Grand, thought Onion, that's him busy for the next few hours.

'Grandad, we're just going to play in the attic!' he called.

'Fine, just stay on the boards and don't fall through the floor,' he shouted back. Some of the attic floor was covered in plywood boards, but a lot of it was just bare rafters with big gaps between them.

Clíona and Dallan were still up there with Róisín. There had been some developments. For a start, Róisín was wearing Derek's phone on a cord around her neck. Onion nearly fainted when he saw it.

'What's . . . what's she doing with Derek's phone?' he wheezed, suddenly needing to take an urgent blast of his inhaler.

'Oh, I thought it was her phone,' Clíona replied.

'Why would an orang-utan have a phone?' Sive asked.

'Well, she has a dress,' Clíona pointed out.

'Those are totally different things!'

'It was keeping her quiet,' Dallan added. 'She squealed if we didn't let her play with it.'

'Oh, I am so dead!' Onion moaned.

'No, wait, look what I did!' Clíona waved them over to show them the device. 'I turned the phone into a translator. It uses the camera and an app to translate Róisín's signing into words. Try it. Ask her something.'

Onion threw his hands up helplessly and turned to the ape. 'Okay. Róisín, how are you feeling today?'

Sive signed the question, in case the ape didn't understand Onion's words. Róisín started to sign, her hands moving quickly, putting her whole face and body into it too. The phone's camera was taking it all in. It took a couple of seconds to process, then a voice like a satnav came from the speaker: 'I AM FEELING VERY AARDVARK SWIMMING POOL.'

'It still needs a bit of work,' Clíona told them.

'No, really?' Onion snorted. He saw he'd hurt his friend's feelings. 'All right, it's still very clever. Thanks for that. But I can't let her keep Derek's phone. He'll have a fit if he doesn't get it back soon. Can't we use your phone for this?'

'I suppose,' Clíona replied. 'But it's back at my house. I strapped it to our robot hoover. I wanted to film what it does when we're not there. Oh, I oiled the hinges of the attic hatch too.'

Róisín, holding on protectively to the phone, shuffled away and perched on a box.

Onion pushed his glasses up and rubbed his wonky eye, then looked around the attic. 'Hey, have you guys been tidying up?'

'That was Róisín,' Dallan told him. 'She's a neat freak. You heard how Forester nags her about it. Everything has to be stacked nice and tidy or put away in boxes.'

'Except now we'll never be able to find anything up here.' Onion sighed. 'And I have to explain how all the coats ended up in the dishwasher. Obviously, Róisín picked them up off the floor, but she didn't know where they were supposed to go, so she hid them wherever she could. We have to be careful. We don't want this whole thing turning into another cat-in-the-National-Gallery story.'

Everyone turned to stare at Dallan.

'That's not fair,' he complained. 'I did not kidnap that cat. It was just *resting* in my bag.'

'We need a proper plan for tonight,' Sive said, bringing them back to their main problem. 'How are we going to break Maya out? And where do we take her? I don't think we can keep two apes hidden up here.'

They went into a huddle, keeping their voices low.

'We need to find someone who's an expert on orang-utans and get some advice,' Onion said. 'But we can't let them know we have one in our attic. Clíona, you'd be best at that. Dallan, you need to come up with a way to draw Forester and his lot away from Maya's trailer. Sive, we need you to talk to Maya so she knows what's going on, so you'll have to come with me when I sneak into her trailer. We'll have to bring a hacksaw in case she's chained up.'

'What about Róisín?' Clíona asked.

'She'll have to stay here,' Onion said, shaking his head. 'We can't risk taking her with us. If someone spots her, she could wreck everything.'

'No, I mean, where's she gone now?' Clíona said. 'She's not here.'

They all stared at the box the ape had been sitting on. Only a few steps from it, the hatch was still wide open.

'Aw, jaypers!' Onion whined. 'I've gotta remember to close that hatch.'

CHAPTER ELEVEN:

— DEREK'S PHONE

Róisín was in the kitchen, watching Grandad Paddy 'fix' the sink. The four Five O's crept down the stairs and found her there, sitting on the kitchen counter beside the fruit bowl, munching on a banana. Grandad hadn't seen her because the open cupboard door blocked his view.

BANG.

'Bloomin' sink!'

BANG.

'Disgraceful.'

BANG.

'Stupid pipes!' Grandad shouted as he banged under the sink with his rubber mallet.

'Keep cool,' Dallan said quietly to the others. 'If she gets a fright, she might make a noise and he'll see her.'

They silently beckoned to the ape, trying to get her to come out to the hallway. Róisín waved to them and dropped to the floor, but instead of coming out to them, she crouched down beside the open toolbox. She started poking around in it. Onion shook his head at her frantically.

'Is that you, Onion?' Grandad said without looking out from under the sink. 'Hand us that that pipe wrench, will yeh? It's the—'

Róisín took a tool from the box and handed it round the cupboard door.

'Good lad,' Grandad said, taking it from her. 'I didn't think you even knew what a pipe wrench was! Maybe you can give me a hand more often, eh?'

'Sure, Grandad,' Onion said, scooting up to Róisín and picking her up. 'I'll just be upstairs if you need anything else, okay?'

'Right so. Stick on the kettle, will yeh? Think it's about time for a cup of tea.'

Clíona was already there, clicking the kettle on as Onion, heaving a huge, relieved breath, carried the orang-utan back to where the others were waiting just outside the kitchen. They stared in disbelief, and Sive gently closed the kitchen door after Onion came through.

'Oh, my heart, that was close!' Dallan gasped. Róisín signed a question. The phone quickly translated: **'PLEASE CAN I HAVE MORE TOILET BRUSH?'**

'She means bananas,' Sive said. 'Stupid phone apps.'

'I guessed that,' Onion whispered. 'Keep your voices down. Let's get her back upstairs before anything else happens. I don't think my nerves can take any more of this.'

It was right then, just as he was heading down the hall towards the stairs, that the front door opened and Derek walked in. Standing there in front of him, less than two steps away, was his younger brother, cradling an orang-utan wearing two blue bows in her hair and a pink ballet costume.

Derek's mouth opened, then closed again. Then it opened. And closed again. It opened one more time as he saw what was hanging round the ape's neck.

'THAT'S MY PHONE!' he roared.

CHAPTER ELEVEN: DEREK'S PHONE

Róisín screamed as he lunged towards her, trying to grab the phone. She leapt out of Onion's arms and bounced off the wall, rebounding out past Derek, who crashed into Onion, knocking him flying. In a flash of ginger fur, Róisín vanished out the open front door, scampering round the back of the house. The Five O's gave chase, getting in each other's way as they pushed through the door, with Derek bringing up the rear.

The young ape was up onto the back wall even as the kids came through to the garden. She bounded along the top of the wall, the phone dangling from her neck, to next door's garden and kept going. She was heading for the end of the street, in the opposite direction to the circus, which would take her to another stretch of green. Sive led the way along the wall with Onion following, both of them walking one foot in front of the other, delicately balanced, while Dallan and Clíona headed back out to the street to see if they could sprint down and cut Róisín off at the end of the row of houses.

Derek was taking the shortest straight line to his phone. He hopped up on top of the wall, shoved Onion and Sive off into next door's garden to get them out of his way and hurried with short steps after the escaping orang-utan.

Sive landed on her feet on the grass and was back up on the wall in seconds. Onion landed on his backside against a compost bin, knocking it over. Scrambling through the spill of smelly contents, he had just a few seconds of terror as he realised he was still in his good clothes and shoes for Mass and Granny was going to eat his head off for wrecking them. Then he was back up onto the wall, trying to catch

up with Sive and his brother. They could only move so fast up there, and this slow-motion teetering, tottering chase might have looked more dramatic if Róisín hadn't already reached the end of the row as if she was loping along a flat running track. She jumped off the last wall and disappeared.

Taking the long way round and having to sneak through someone's garden to get to the green, Dallan arrived just as Derek was dropping down onto the grass. They were there in time to see Róisín reach the bottom of an old oak tree and start climbing.

'Oh no!' Dallan groaned as the rest of the gang arrived. 'She's gone up the Trapping Tree!'

This was a disaster. Several trees on the green had been there long before the estates were built – some of them were more than a hundred years old. The Trapping Tree was the stuff of legend. So many games of football had ended when the ball got caught in this tree. What the tree took, it never gave back. In the summer, its thick foliage hid its impenetrable depths, but in the winter, you could see dozens of burst footballs stuck in the branches, never to return except as shapeless, weathered bits of plastic that the tree let fall from time to time like a giant bird's droppings.

Nobody could climb the Trapping Tree. The lowest branches were too high up, and the only attempt to try with a ladder had ended in broken bones. You could throw a stick up to try and get your ball back, but this was merely a reliable way to lose a good stick. No, anything that went up there wasn't coming down until the Trapping Tree was done with it.

'Róisín! Róisín, come on down!' Onion called up desperately. 'Derek didn't mean any harm. He was just worried about his phone. It's okay. Really! We'll get you another phone, I promise! Come on down, Róisín! Nobody wants to hurt you!'

There was a movement up in the thick clumps of leaves, the faintest flicker of ginger fur, then a satnav voice said: 'GO AWAY. YOU ARE TRUMPET ME FEEL BAKED BEANS. I AM STAYING IN THIS WELLY BOOT UNTIL YOU GO.'

'I'm really getting tired of that blinkin' phone,' Sive grumbled.

'Now look what you did!' Onion snapped at Derek.

'What *I* did?' Derek exploded. He grabbed his little brother by the scruff of the neck. 'What was that thing doing in our house? Where did you find her? Why did she have my PHONE? What's she doing with my PHONE? How are you going to get my PHONE back? And have I mentioned that SHE HAS MY PHONE, YOU CLUMP!'

'Stop shouting or we'll never get her down from there!' Sive said, pulling the two brothers apart.

'Get who down from there?' a voice said from behind them.

The Five O's turned to see a beautiful blonde girl standing there, with a brute of a boy at each shoulder. The boys were twins, each of them a head taller than the girl, with mullets of black hair, wide flushed faces and bodies that were only slightly more evolved than Róisín's. Sive rolled her eyes in a 'typical' expression. Onion's wonky eye rolled because that's just what it did when things went down the toilet. As if this situation wasn't bad enough, these three had to show up.

It was Tina Dalton and the Bang-Off-Them Brothers.

CHAPTER TWELVE:

OH NO, NOT TINA DALTON

I f there was anyone who could claim to be the crime boss among the primary school kids of Ballinlud, it would be Tina Dalton. Even some of the secondary school kids were scared of her. Or at least, the smart ones were. Tina had big plans for her future, and most of them had to do with her Being in Charge of Everything.

The Bang-Off-Them Brothers, Barry and Larry Bang, were bad enough, the muscle to Tina's brains, but at least they were the kind of trouble you could see coming. They looked like trouble. And if you didn't see them, you'd probably smell them because the bang off them would knock out a donkey. Which, of course, is where their nickname came from. The thugs were both devoted to Tina, perhaps even in love with her.

Tina was a different matter, a different class of trouble altogether. With big blue eyes, full pouty lips, blonde ringlets cut in a fringe and perfect skin with just a sprinkle of freckles, she looked like a slightly cheeky angel.

CHAPTER TWELVE: OH NO, NOT TINA DALTON

But the thing that stood out most about her was her nose, which she was usually sticking into other people's business. In fact, she sounded like she talked through her nose instead of her mouth, like her nostrils were chewing toffees. She paid attention in class and was a sporty all-rounder too. And wasn't she kind to let those two smelly trogs hang around with her? Grown-ups thought she was a very mature young lady.

Her fellow pupils were scared to be left alone with her.

Now here she was, standing with the Five O's under the Trapping Tree. And she was curious.

'Hey, Derek,' she said.

'Hey, Tina.' He gave her a careful nod.

Derek was in secondary school, so she showed him a bit more respect than the others, and he always tried to be cool around her. She was nearly a year older than Onion, but a year and a half younger than Derek. He was starting to take an interest in girls, but taking an interest in Tina

Dalton was like stepping into a tiger's cage to see if it was hungry.

'So . . . get who down from there?' she asked the gang again. And she expected an answer.

'Yeah, get who down?' Barry Bang repeated. He found it hard to put words together on his own but was always happy to repeat Tina's demands.

'It's our cat,' Dallan, the fastest mouth in the Five O's, replied. 'She's stuck up the tree.'

'Jaypers, Dallan, you didn't kidnap another cat, did ya?' Tina laughed.

'That cat was just *resting* in my bag!' he retorted, scowling defensively.

'It's my cat,' Sive said sullenly, chewing her gum extra slowly. 'It's no big deal – she just ran up the tree and she won't come down.'

'Whatever. Yawn.' Tina didn't actually yawn: she just said the word. 'I'm here on business. Dinesh from Dundeer, ya know, Dundeer Dinesh, has challenged my Ballinlud crew to a basketball match. Thing is, I'm two players short. So I'm bringing on my subs. That'll be you two.' She pointed at Sive and Dallan. 'You'll wait for my call and come running when I tell you.'

'We're not in your "crew",' Sive told her, her voice just a little bit nervous.

'Yeah, we don't take orders from you,' Dallan said to back her up.

'Sure you do,' Tina said confidently. 'Everyone does eventually.'

She was too sharp not to pick up on the mood of the Five O's. There was more going on here than a cat stuck in a tree. She raised her gaze to the foliage above her, peering into the green gloom to see what there was to see. Something ginger moved up there, barely visible in the clutter of leaves.

'Barry, Larry,' she said. 'You're going to climb that tree and get that cat.'

The brothers eyed each other nervously.

'That's the Trapping Tree,' Larry said. Pointing out the obvious was an effort for him, but he managed it.

'I realise that,' she replied in a cold voice. 'Now get up there and fetch down that cat.'

'Really, there's no need,' Sive insisted. 'She'll come down eventually.'

'It's okay – it's no bother, really,' Tina said, smiling sweetly.

Then, her face changing to an expression of utter seriousness, she glared at the twins and jerked her head towards the tree.

Onion had often thought there were advantages to being stupid, especially if you also had no imagination. For a start, you were less likely to be scared of doing stupid things. It also meant you probably left all your thinking to other people. The Bang-Off-Them Brothers did whatever Tina told them because years of training had ensured it never occurred to them not to do it. So if Tina told them to climb a tree that couldn't be climbed, then up they'd go. And so, up they went.

CHAPTER TWELVE: OH NO, NOT TINA DALTON

The Five O's watched with fearful fascination. There was nothing else they could do to object. Neither Bang brother was tall enough to reach the lower branches, so one had to stand on the other's shoulders. This meant an argument to see who was to do the climbing and who was to get stood on. Barry ended up on the bottom after Tina lost patience with them and issued further instructions. Larry clambered clumsily onto his brother's shoulders. Tall as they were, Larry was still too short to reach the lowest branch. He'd have to jump for it.

He lunged upwards, causing Barry to grunt in pain, and with his short, strong fingers, Larry managed to grab hold of the branch. Barry moved aside to watch. It was right at that moment that a burst football flew down and smacked Larry in the face, tearing his grip free and sending him plummeting to the ground. He landed hard on his back, the air thumped out of his lungs. He lay there, wheezing and whimpering, trying to breathe.

Tina showed no sympathy. Squinting up into the branches again, she had a suspicious expression on her face. 'You said that's a cat up there?' she asked in a flat voice.

'Definitely,' Onion replied. 'But she's a really big cat.'

Tina prodded Larry with her toe. 'Right, you give the boost up this time. Barry, you're climbing.'

The twins responded with mindless obedience. With Larry still struggling to breathe, the pair moved to the tree again, and this time Barry climbed up onto his brother's shoulders. Another football shot down, whacking him on the head even before he could reach for the branch. He gasped and clutched his head, looking down at Tina. Then a third ball struck him on the side of his head, a stinging impact to his ear, and he toppled off Larry's shoulders and crashed down on the grass. He let out a long, pained whine and then a cough.

'A cat,' Tina said. 'You're telling me a cat threw those balls?'

'She's probably just knocking them loose,' Onion told her. 'I don't think she's going to come down while you're here. She's not good with strangers. Just leave us to it, and she'll come back to us eventually.'

High in the sky above them, something buzzed past. It was a drone, making a sweeping turn. It flew past again and then disappeared. All the kids watched it fade into the distance over the houses, wondering where it had come from.

'It's like it was looking for something,' Clíona commented.

Something else flew down from the tree and bounced off the roots, breaking apart. It wasn't a football. It was too soft and brown and stank way too much to be anything made for sport. It was poo. And it sure wasn't poo from any cat Tina had ever seen, unless there was a leopard or a tiger up there.

Her eyes narrowed and the others could see she was thinking this through. She didn't want to hang about here all day with poo dropping around her. It wouldn't be cool. And if it was true that the 'cat' didn't like strangers, then that's what she'd end up doing. But like all liars, Tina assumed that everyone else lied all the time too, so she was sure the Five O's were up to something. Though, in fairness to her, she was right.

'On your feet, Barry,' she snapped. 'This is getting boring. Let's head down to the shopping centre. Good luck with your "cat", guys. Hope you get her back soon.'

And with that, she walked off, the two ogres trotting along behind her. The Five O's watched her go, then they all gazed up into the tree, uncertain what they should do next.

'We need fruit,' Clíona said, 'to attract her down. She hasn't eaten in ages – she'll be hungry and thirsty.'

'Good idea,' Onion said, 'but it's also a problem. We've got to find a way of feeding her and Maya. I've already taken more fruit than Granny can believe. Me and Derek don't really eat the stuff. She's going to get very suspicious if I take any more.'

'Who's Maya?' Derek asked.

'She's the Great Orangini,' Onion replied.

'The Great Orangini is a man, ya sap.'

'No. He's a she, and she's an orang-utan.'

'What's going on?' Derek said, scratching his head.

'Róisín's mam,' Onion replied. 'We're going to break her out of the circus tonight. Then we're going to help them live out here, in the wild, in Ballinlud.'

'Oh sure, right. Of course.' Derek frowned and nodded earnestly, as if this was a completely normal thing to be talking about.

'We can all chip in,' Sive spoke up. 'Between the four of us, we can get a lot more fruit. And we can buy some too.'

Derek made a funny little noise, drew in a really deep breath and then, 'What are you talkin' about?' he shouted at them, with an exasperated expression. 'None of yiz have any sense at all, do yiz? Not a clue. Nickin' fruit from your fruit bowls to feed that ape? Have you seen what a big dog eats in a week? Every week? And you want to keep her mother too? She'd be, like, human-sized, right? Have you any idea how much food you're talking about, you dopey bunch of curtain cacks? Our Granny would have to buy a week's worth of fruit every single day. Even if all four of you chipped in, d'ya think your folks wouldn't notice you'd all become fruit freaks? Yiz are all hopeless.'

This dose of reality hit the Five O's hard, but especially Onion because Derek gave him one of his signature dead arms. Their faces dropped.

CHAPTER TWELVE: OH NO, NOT TINA DALTON

Onion rubbed the sore spot on his arm, Sive chewed her gum harder, Dallan took his thick glasses off and cleaned them with the edge of his shirt and Clíona's expression went blank, which it did when she was trying not to think too hard. In their hearts, they knew he was right. They had no way of gathering that much fruit together, over and over again, without their parents getting suspicious.

'What you need to do,' Derek said to them, in a more patient tone, 'is start raiding some bins. And don't look at me like that. Yes, I have to admit it – having a couple of orang-utans around would be all kinds of cool.'

CHAPTER THIRTEEN:
THE BIN RAID

Derek explained how it worked. Supermarkets sold fresh food, which they dumped in the garbage when it went out of date. This included any fruit which wasn't all that fresh any more or had got a bit bruised. It was a massive waste, but people expected their food to be shiny and new all the time and the shops didn't have anywhere else to put the stuff that was old, battered or just plain ugly. But most of it was still edible, and what would an orang-utan care if their apple or banana had a few bruises?

The local SuperPrice were always dumping fresh fruit and veg in their bins, and since they clearly didn't want it any more, they wouldn't be bothered if someone took a load of it off their hands. All the Five O's had to do was raid the bins every few days, and they'd have all the food they needed to feed their apes.

'How do you know all this?' Sive asked.

'I heard it from Candy Dan,' Derek told her. 'He steals out-of-date cakes from the bins every weekend. Some of them are *really* out of date. He brings them to school with his lunch.'

This caused a few green faces, though everyone also wondered if the possibility of an endless supply of free cake would be worth the risk of vomiting to death from food poisoning. Getting down to business, they agreed that right now maybe wasn't the best time to go rescuing wasted fruit from bins, but they needed to have food for when they broke Maya out tonight, and Dallan argued that there'd be guards out everywhere once word got out that The Great Orangini had gone missing. They had to do this now, before the heat came down on Ballinlud.

'Okay, might as well get started,' Onion said. 'Derek, it's good to have you on board.'

'Don't go gettin' ideas,' Derek responded. 'I'll help you with this one thing, but I'm still not in your stupid gang.'

'Sure thing.' Onion nodded. 'Sive, you and Clíona actually eat fruit, so you know what's good. You can go with Derek to raid the bins. Me and Dallan will stay and keep watch for Róisín.'

'You will in me barney!' Sive snorted. 'You and Dallan have only got one decent eye between you, and it's covered with a patch. I'm the only one who can sign, so I'll have to stay with Róisín. Derek has to show you where the bins are. Dallan can stay with me. If Róisín runs again, we need the fastest ones to go after her.'

They couldn't argue with her logic, so that was that. The O'Brien brothers were still in their good clothes after Mass, but there was nothing to be done about that now. The chase across the back gardens had already done damage. If they showed up back at the house in this state, Granny would be hopping mad and might not let them out again. A bit more mess from the garbage wouldn't make much difference in the long run. Derek led Onion and Clíona across the green to an alley that took them down to the back wall of SuperPrice. Climbing over, they dropped into a yard that contained stacked pallets, a couple of delivery vans, a forklift and a row of industrial wheelie bins.

'Ah jaypers, we didn't bring any bags to carry the fruit,' Onion whispered, slapping his head as they approached the bins. 'What are we gonna do?'

Derek found a clump of 'bags for life' stuffed down a pocket beside the seat on the forklift, and Onion wondered if he knew more than he was telling about raiding bins. Anyway, now they had bags. Derek showed them which bin had the fruit and veg, swinging the lid up so it was leaning against the wall of the building.

'Okay, I'll keep watch,' he said softly. 'You two do the digging.'

'Why aren't you helping?' Onion argued.

'Because she's YOUR ape. And she has MY PHONE. Up a tree,' Derek said, a little too loudly. 'Now make like wasps and get into the bin before I deck yiz with this bunch of bananas,' Derek said, shaking his fist at them.

Onion and Clíona leaned over the bin. There was a smell, a sweet, sickening smell. Not that the food in the bin was all rotten – the bin was just well used and had seen a lot of old stock. Onion and Clíona wanted the best they could get for Róisín and her mother, so they had to dig around

in the mass of fruit and vegetables to pull out the most edible pieces.

Onion decided he needed to get into the bin to reach the really choice bits. He only realised his mistake when he sank in up to his shins and felt wet soaking through his socks. Groaning, he started handing apples, oranges, pears and peaches out to Clíona, as well as tomatoes and vegetables that didn't seem too disgusting. When they had two fairly full bags, Onion went to climb out. There was gunk on his feet and he slipped on the rim of the wheelie bin and toppled back in, jolting the bin. The lid fell shut with a bang, hitting him on the head and thumping him down into the smelly contents.

'Ah!' he gasped, spitting bits of fruit pulp out of his mouth. Bright lights burst in his vision and he howled in pain, clutching his skull. 'What— Jaypers! Sweet janey, me head!'

Sprawled there stunned among all the mushed fruit and vegetables, he cried a little bit and wheezed until he took a puff of his inhaler. It took him a minute or two to cop that he'd been lying there in the darkness with just the daylight glowing through the grey plastic of the huge bin. Why had Clíona not opened the lid to check on him?

Then he heard the shouting. And the running feet. And the shouting. Getting up and carefully lifting the lid, he peered out. Clíona was sprinting for the wall with Derek a few paces ahead of her, each of them carrying a bag of fruit. One of the guys from the shop was belting after them – he even followed them over the wall. A woman was jogging after him, her phone to her ear as she made a call. No doubt The Ferg and Garda Judge were on their way.

Onion wouldn't make it to the wall – he was cut off. And that woman might turn and look in the bin at any moment to figure out what they'd been up to. There was only one thing for it. Raising the lid a bit higher, he slipped over the side of the bin and crept into the open back door of the supermarket.

CHAPTER THIRTEEN: THE BIN RAID

He found himself in the storeroom, surrounded by racks of crates, boxes and containers of stock ready to be unpacked and brought out to the shelves. Trying to act natural, he headed for the doorway that led out onto the shop floor.

Out in the aisles, he continued to act casual, like he was just there to shop. People stared at him without trying to be obvious about it.

'Hello there, Mrs Byrne,' he said, nodding to one of the neighbours from his street.

'Hello, Onion,' she said from behind her shopping trolley, a look of puzzlement on her face. 'Say hi to your granny for me, will yeh?'

'I will of course.'

'I don't usually see you here without her, Onion?' enquired the nosey neighbour.

'Ohhh, just picking up some fruit and veg that she forgot,' answered Onion.

'Well, I think you have enough fruit and veg on your clothes there for tonight's dinner,' remarked Mrs Byrne.

'Haha, right so.' Onion laughed awkwardly as he escaped down the vegetable aisle towards the exit.

He caught sight of his reflection in a mirror behind the coffee machine near the tills as he passed. A pathetic little whimper escaped from his mouth. He'd been so intent on his escape, he hadn't noticed the state of his clothes and shoes. His good Mass shirt and trousers were absolutely covered in smeared pieces of banana and tomato and avocado and all sorts of other stuff. It was all over him, mashed into his hair, and his shoes and socks were soaked in it. And he stank to high heaven. He'd never be able to clean this off. He'd have to walk home like this, past all the neighbours' houses.

Forget about getting in trouble with the guards. Granny was going to kill him.

CHAPTER FOURTEEN:
GRANNY THROWS A WOBBLER

As it turned out, Onion showing up at home looking like he'd gone swimming in a fruit smoothie was the perfect diversion to keep Granny and Grandad busy while the Five O's got Róisín back up to his bedroom. Róisín had needed little persuasion to come down from the Trapping Tree once she saw the two big bags of fruit. Back at the house, Grandad was still under the sink, hard at work, having recently finished a fourth cup of tea. Granny, as luck would have it, was putting on some laundry.

Onion took a deep breath, as if he was about to plunge into the freezing cold sea at an Irish beach, and stepped into the kitchen. Granny was shutting the washing machine door. She turned the dial, hit the button, looked round and her mouth opened wide, releasing a kind of strangled hissing sound as her eyes fell on her grandson. She pointed at his Mass clothes, unable to speak for a moment, and then her first words were:

'Arghhh! Arghhhhhh! Arghhh!'

Granny just pointed and screamed at the stains on Onion's clothes. 'Look at your clothes! There are stains on stains on stains on stains! How am I going to get them out? This is worse than the table cloth,' she said in horror.

Onion had to take his clothes off right there in the kitchen while Granny subjected him to a barrage of guilt, fury and embarrassment.

'All the things we do for you and all I ask is that you try and be respectable sometimes especially on Sundays when everyone's home and watching and what were you doing rolling in a compost heap Paddy will you look at the state of him what are we going to do with you at all there's no helping you these stains will never come out and heavens above the smell I can't believe this what possessed you Onion have you lost your senses sometimes I wonder what goes through your head . . .'

And so on, and so on. Her voice was at a pitch that would have cracked glass, and it seemed to go on for hours, though it was probably only a couple of minutes.

Eventually, Onion was able to climb the stairs, dressed only in his underpants, get to his room and put on some fresh clothes. The rest of the gang were there and gave him sympathetic looks. He was nearly in tears; he hated upsetting his granny almost as much as he hated being given out to. Derek had changed too and was trying to take his phone back off the ape. After a few attempts that resulted in Róisín squealing in protest, he gave up and slumped on his bed with his back against the wall, sulking.

Clíona had a piece of paper and a pencil and was drawing the layout of the circus tents and vehicles. It was time to start planning Maya's escape. Róisín watched with interest, munching on a juicy orange, though the others weren't sure she understood what was happening. Every now and then, Sive turned to sign some questions to the orang-utan, who answered as best she could.

It would start getting dark about eight or nine. Onion and Derek were supposed to be in bed by ten. Their grandparents were strict about bedtime on a school night. Two shows were advertised for that evening, one at half-past six and one at nine. They decided to make their move around half eight, between the end of the first show and the start of the second one. Maya would be in her trailer. If she was in chains, Onion said, they'd have to saw them off.

'You can't saw through chains that easily. It'd take for ever,' Derek told them, shaking his head at their ignorance. 'Have you never tried to saw through a bike lock?'

'No,' Sive said. 'When did you try to saw through a bike lock? And why?'

'I . . . It was just . . . I lost the key!' he said defensively. 'It was for *my* bike. Anyway, it's the same thing. If she's chained to something to stop her running away, you'll need the key. We won't be able to break anything solid enough to hold an orang-utan.'

'Róisín, do you know where Forester keeps the key to the chains?' Onion asked the ape.

Róisín put two fingers to her temple and shook her head to sign she didn't understand.

'YOU HAVE NO BRAIN IN MY HEAD,' the phone said.

Sive swore in exasperation and muted it. She repeated the question in sign. It took a minute to explain what a 'key' was. Then Róisín got it. The ape motioned with her hands.

Sive groaned. 'Truck normally has it,' she translated.

Everyone else groaned then too. Truck, the woman built like a professional wrestler. Who looked like she could crunch you into a bundle with her bare hands and play basketball with you. How would they get the key from her?

'And then there's where we're going to put them after we break Maya out,' Onion said in a worried voice. 'Sooner or later, Granny and Grandad are going to cop that we have an ape in the house.'

'Oh, I forgot to tell you, I've found someone who knows a lot about orang-utans,' Clíona told them. 'I did a search while I was setting up the translator on the phone.'

'On *my* phone,' Derek grunted. 'I swear, I'm going to have no credit left at all.'

'You know Tota Freedom Wildlife Park in Wicklow?' Clíona continued. 'The place is owned by Doctor Michelle Michaels and Major Mike Michaels. And they're primatologists.'

'They're what?' Dallan asked.

'They study monkeys and apes. They actually have orang-utans in the park.'

'If they keep orang-utans in the park . . .' Onion began.

'They might let Maya and Róisín live there?' Clíona suggested.

'. . . they could tell us how to help them live in Ballinlud,' Onion finished.

'I think Clíona's idea is better,' Derek said, eyeing his phone.

'No, Róisín and Maya stay with us!' Onion insisted. Granny's outburst had left him shaken and he looked ready to cry again. 'Ballinlud is their home now.'

Everyone looked out the window again, at the street of identical semi-detached houses, surrounded by many more streets of very similar semi-detached houses.

'Whatever,' Derek muttered.

'So what we're saying is,' Dallan said, trying to sum up what had been decided so far, 'we have to keep Róisín here for the rest of the day without your grandparents finding out, then we have to go to the circus, create a diversion that draws all the circus people away from Maya, while also stealing the key to Maya's chains from that monster of a woman, Truck. Then we have to free Maya and bring her back here or somewhere else. We have to hide both apes from the circus people and the guards, then we have to contact these . . . these . . .'

'Primatologists,' Clíona supplied.

'. . . primatologists and, without them finding out that we have, you know, a pair of orang-utans, we have to learn how to look after orang-utans for . . . for the rest of their lives?'

Everyone turned to look at Onion.

'In a nutshell, yes,' he said.

CHAPTER FIFTEEN:
—
A GATHERING OF VILLAINS

Without the glitzy lighting, most of the Big Top was in shadow. Standing in those shadows was Joe Forester, flanked by Truck and Bucket. Bucket was using his phone to fly a drone around the maze of struts and cables at the top of the tent. When Tina Dalton and the Bang-Off-Them Brothers walked in, the girl cast her gaze around suspiciously, noting the drone in the air above her, before nodding a cautious greeting to the ringmaster.

It was rare to see such a gathering of fiendish villainy in the very ordinary Dublin suburb of Ballinlud.

'You wanted to meet?' Tina said, getting right down to business.

'Thank you for coming,' Forester replied, moving a bit closer. 'Word on the street is that this is your territory. Anything that happens with the kids round here has to be run through you. Is my information correct?'

'That's what they say.' Tina wasn't about to admit to anything directly, in case Forester was working with the cops and he was wired to record this. 'What's it to you?'

'I've lost something,' the ringmaster said, starting to walk in a slow circle around the three children. 'Something of great personal value. A beloved pet has gone missing. She and I have a deep emotional bond and it would break my heart if something was to happen to her.'

'Sure,' Tina said, suspecting that Forester had neither emotional bonds nor a heart, but what did that matter to her? 'So is the heat involved?'

'The "heat"?' Forester repeated as he walked around them. 'No, no, the guards are not involved. This is a delicate matter. I would prefer to keep the "heat" out of it. Which is why I'd like to enlist your help.'

Tina didn't like having him behind her, but she didn't want to look nervous either, so she didn't turn to watch him as he circled them. And she was nervous. Forester was a whole other level of nasty. And though the twin brothers were big and strong for their age, that wrestler woman and that sinewy trapeze artist looked like hard-core professional thugs. Also, they were grown-ups and she and the boys weren't even teenagers yet. She knew her limits.

'What are you offering?' she asked.

'A reward,' he said. 'One hundred euros for information that leads to the capture of the animal.'

Tina was twelve years old. A hundred euros was in the big league. With that kind of money she could hire a couple of ace basketball players for her team – there were two girls in Tallum who were unbeatable. She could finally take Dundeer Dinesh down! She kept her cool.

'I'll do it for one fifty,' she said.

'One twenty-five,' he countered.

'Okay, you've got a deal. So what is this thing? A dog? A cat? A rat?'

'A rat! Very droll.' Forester chuckled coldly as he continued in his circle, ending it standing just a couple of paces in front her and leaning his face in close to hers. 'No. It's an orang-utan.'

Tina waited to see if he was joking. He wasn't. 'You've got an orang-utan wandering around Ballinlud and you can't find it?' She wanted to laugh in his face, and she would have if he was one of the saddo kids she spent her life around, but she thought that laughing at Joe Forester might not be a good idea.

'It's a "she", and I think someone might be hiding her,' he said.

The drone buzzed by overhead and Tina had a sudden flashback. Onion and Derek and their gang of pathetic friends hanging around the bottom of the Trapping Tree with their fake casual act. The glimpse of ginger fur among the leaves. The 'cat' that could throw footballs. This would be the easiest hundred and twenty-five quid she'd ever make. She didn't tell Forester, though, because she assumed he'd try and cheat her out of her money. After all, it was what she would do if she was him.

'It's as good as done,' she told him. 'I'll bring your ape in myself.'

'Just her whereabouts will do fine,' Forester assured her. 'We'll do the rest.'

Tina held her hand out and he shook it firmly.

'One more thing,' she said. Nodding towards Truck, she asked, 'Where can I get me one of those?'

'Oh, I breed them,' he answered. 'Truck was born in Antrim, trained in powerlifting in Russia, then years of clown school in France. She is my masterpiece. And way out of your price range, young lady.' He motioned dismissively to the twin brothers. 'These oafs will serve you well enough for now. Come back to me in a few years, when you've built up your operation, and I'll provide you with some proper henchpeople. That's if you're serious about making the big time, of course.'

'Oh, you'd better believe it,' she said, with a wicked villain's grin. 'I'm going all the way to the top!'

CHAPTER SIXTEEN:

—

JUST GET THROUGH THE DAY

The Five O's were facing a couple of problems with their plan to break Maya out of the circus. First, Onion was grounded until further notice because of what he'd done to his Mass clothes. No going out and early to bed. Derek was also grounded because Granny and Grandad suspected he had something to with what had happened to Onion, and in their house, suspicion was nine-tenths of the law.

Second, they had hours to wait, and keeping an orang-utan happy enough that she would stay quiet and not look to wander around was a tricky business. They didn't try to keep her up in the attic because they'd attract too much attention climbing in and out of there, even with the hatch's freshly oiled hinges, so they stayed in Onion's room.

Clíona went home and took her phone off her robot hoover, so at least Róisín could now use that as a translator, and Derek got his phone back. Clíona was gradually improving the app's woeful performance. Obviously they didn't need it when Sive was around, as she was much better at translating anyway, but the phone's voice also helped cover up Róisín's hoots, yelps and squeals as she played.

Onion often spent time with his little sister on Sundays, and Molly had noticed that he was ignoring her, so she kept trying to get into the boys' room. Eventually, he had to come out and play with her dolls to distract her from the strange ape sounds coming from his bedroom, which had Molly madly curious.

'What's that noise!' Molly said as she pointed at the bedroom.

'Ah, it's just a game the guys are playing in there,' said Onion.

'I want to go in and play,' said Molly.

'Hey, look, a spider!' shouted Onion, trying to distract her. Molly loved spiders.

'Yes, spider! Hello, spider,' she said as she chased it. Even having eight legs can't help you escape when Molly wants to play with you.

Meanwhile, the others kept Róisín busy. She liked games. She liked Peekaboo and dropping stuff on the floor so someone had to pick it up. Her favourite thing was playing catch with a tennis ball.

Oh, and she loved having her hair brushed. All of it. The room was soon covered in ginger ape hair. She was very restless, and it was a constant effort to keep her from wanting to get out. Eventually, she settled down on Onion's bed for a nap and the gang sighed in relief. Everyone agreed that it was cool having their own ape, but it was like having a baby: it was a lot of work. Róisín needed her mother.

'Do you think if they lived in the trees on the green they could stay hidden out there?' Clíona asked.

'Not in winter,' Sive said. 'Those trees aren't evergreen. There'd be no leaves.'

'I think we'd have to let them loose up in the mountains,' Dallan said. Ballinlud was close to the Dublin Mountains. 'They'd have proper space out there, and we could cycle out to visit them.'

'Brilliant, just brilliant,' Derek said sourly, staring at his phone screen. 'I've run out of credit. Thanks a lot, you guzzers.'

CHAPTER SIXTEEN: JUST GET THROUGH THE DAY

One major aspect for the O'Brien boys of life with their grandparents was that, within those walls, they were effectively living in the 1980s. Derek's phone was the only computer in the house and it ran on pay-as-you-go credit, which used up most of his pocket money. There was no Wi-Fi in the house because there was no modem. They had a phone plugged into the wall with a handset that was still attached to the base with one of those twisty cords. 'Read a book,' Grandad would say. The closest thing they had to the Internet was the ancient thirty-book set of Encyclopædia Britannica they had in the cupboard under the stairs. Clíona loved them. Grandad had pulled the books out of a skip at a job he'd been on years ago.

This was the downside for the gang of hanging around the O'Briens' house. More freedom, but no technology. Sive's parents were 'in business' and had plenty of money. They were the strictest of all the parents, but she had loads of cool stuff, just no phone. Clíona's mother was single, a scientist who loved tech and gadgets as much as her daughter. Dallan's parents both had normal jobs in the county council, and though he didn't have a phone, he had a tablet and an Xbox.

Derek had once found a computer in a box in the attic. You had to load games onto it with tape cassettes. Not DVDs. Not even CDs . . . tape cassettes. There were dinosaur bones that were younger than this computer. Just loading one game took about half an hour and it screamed in pain the whole time it was doing it. There was a black and white TV in the kitchen, but it had a coat hanger for an aerial. Grandad liked to watch snooker on it while he was fixing stuff in there, but he moaned constantly because he had no idea which colour ball was going into which pocket. Granny would tell him to go into the living room and watch it on the big colour TV, but he loved a good moan almost as much as he loved clowns, so he insisted on watching snooker on the black and white TV every weekend.

CHAPTER SIXTEEN: JUST GET THROUGH THE DAY

As well as the TV there was a microwave oven in the kitchen, which Granny talked about as if it was some kind of NASA-built artificial intelligence, but it was so old Derek was convinced it gave off radiation like a nuclear reactor every time it was used. He wouldn't go close to it while it was on. It heated food to volcanic temperatures on one part of the plate but left it cold in other spots, and when it was running, the hum was like a ship's engine.

There was no point in the whole gang staying in the bedroom all the time, so they took shifts. Some of them had to stay downstairs making noise to help cover up the sounds Róisín was making. Onion got a break from Molly when Sive offered to play with the dolls. Clíona went home again to use her beloved Wi-Fi to do some research on keeping orang-utans. Dallan engaged Granny in conversation about the goings-on of the neighbours. He had the gift of the gab and could talk polite rubbish for hours, a vital skill when dealing with grown-ups. He actually enjoyed it too.

Derek went into the sitting-room with Sive and Molly, sulking because he had no money to buy more phone credit. He watched Formula 1 on the telly with the volume as loud as he dared, occasionally doing funny voices for Molly and her dolls.

Grandad had taken cover behind his newspaper in his armchair, his feet in a basin of hot water. He was aware, on some level, that there was more than the usual fuss going on around him and was grumbling to himself about the state of the world.

'Bloomin' water charges. I mean, who owns water? It's like having a mountain charge.'

Onion stayed up in his room with Róisín, who was still asleep on his bed. The events of the last couple of days and a bad night's sleep were catching up on him, and he started getting drowsy himself. Taking off his glasses, he blinked his good left eye and stretched out on the bed with his hands behind his head. He'd just relax for a bit, while everything was under control.

And of course, he fell asleep.

CHAPTER SEVENTEEN:
SOMETHING ELSE TO DO

O nion jumped up in his bed. How long had he been asleep? He had no idea if it was ten minutes or ten hours. Where was Róisín? How had Granny or Grandad not seen the ape? How had his friends not seen the ape? He whimpered to himself and felt a terrible urge to pee.

He walked really carefully, as if making noise would suddenly cause the orang-utan to appear in front of his grandparents. Peering into the sitting-room, he saw Dallan and Sive sitting on the sofa next to Derek, watching a property programme called Houses You'll Never Be Able to Buy. Molly wasn't there. Onion figured that *Molly must have found something else to do.* Grandad was still in there behind his newspaper, his feet in a freshly steaming basin of water.

Onion didn't disturb them. He noticed the coats were back on the stand in the hall. Granny was, no doubt, still wondering who'd put them in the dishwasher. If Róisín was wandering around, she might start tidying up again, putting things in odd spots, though nothing looked out of place . . .

Róisín wasn't in the kitchen either. A peek in told him Granny had been baking again. As she waited on whatever was in the oven, she sat at the table reading a book entitled *I See Ghosts: Tales from the Grim Peeper.*

The smell of brown bread wafted to his nostrils, making his mouth water. Even so, his throat was very dry and he decided to get a glass of milk. He went into the kitchen and over to the fridge, opened it and shoved his fist in his mouth to stop himself from screaming.

Sitting on the shelves of the fridge, staring out at him with their beady eyes, was a selection of Molly's dolls and teddies. He chewed on his knuckles and made a few small noises in his throat before looking over at Granny.

Molly must have found something else to do.

Holding his breath to stop himself gasping for air, he quickly gathered the toys, knocked the fridge door closed with his bum and hurried out of the kitchen. Then, with fear in his heart, he climbed the stairs and poked his head into Molly's small bedroom.

Róisín was sitting in the tiny bit of space on the floor beside the bed, with Molly standing in front of her, using face-paints to add 'make-up' to the ape's features. It made the young orang-utan look like an absolute nutter. To add to the madness, Róisín was painting Molly's face too. It was hard to tell who was worse. Both of them looked like somebody had fired paints out of a slingshot onto their heads.

'Onion, look at the hairy girl monkey. I have a hairy girl monkey!' she said in a delighted voice.

'Yes, you do. That's great, Molly!' Onion said in a matching tone, his heart beating so fast it was like a motorbike engine. 'Hahaaa, yes. I was keeping the hairy girl monkey as a surprise for you, but, hey, you found her. I mean, you REALLY found her,' Onion said through gritted teeth, wondering how he was going to stop Molly telling everyone. 'Her name's Róisín. Do you like her?'

'She said she would go to my playschool with me. I'm going to bring her to show my friends.'

Onion crouched down beside his little sister and grinned at her. 'No, listen, we have to keep her a secret. We can't even tell Granny or Grandad, okay? They might get annoyed. Róisín's not supposed to be here. She's hiding from some bad men.'

Sive, who had been wondering where Molly had got to, appeared at the bedroom door behind him and slapped a hand over her face as she saw the scene inside. Onion put a finger to his lips and waved her back out.

'But I want to show her to my friends!' Molly repeated. She was getting that pre-tantrum look on her face, when she wanted her way and was letting everyone know there'd be trouble if she didn't get it.

Onion bit his lip and put on his most reasonable face. He was dealing with high explosives here. 'It's just for a while. It's a secret. Just you and me know. And Derek. And my friends. It's to keep her safe. Some mean grown-ups are looking for her and we're going to help her get away from them. Don't you want to help?'

Molly stared earnestly at him and nodded. Róisín nodded too, her big, watery eyes fixed on Onion's wonky one.

'Great, great,' Onion said. 'I think we need to get her up to the attic where no one can see her. Want to help us?'

'Oh yeah, sure,' Molly said, her fingers twisting the brown hair over her ear.

'Great, thanks.'

'And then tomorrow we can take her into playschool so I can show my friends.'

Sive and Molly sat down with Róisín and used some wipes to clean the paint off her face and then played at fixing the bows in her hair. Onion, his nerves in tatters, headed downstairs to talk to Derek. They needed a plan to get them out of the house that evening without their grandparents finding out, all while Róisín stayed good and quiet up in the attic. This circus break-out job was starting to look harder every time he thought about it.

He reached the bottom of the stairs, glanced out the window beside the front door and stopped dead in his tracks. Standing outside, just across the street, were the Bang-Off-Them Brothers. The twins were staring over at the house, all stupid and scary and looking like trouble.

'Ah, now,' Onion groaned. 'What's all this?'

The doorbell rang, making him jump. He opened it to find Tina Dalton standing in the porch. She didn't mess about with small talk.

'I know you have an orang-utan,' she said. Onion went to deny it, but she held up her hand. 'Don't bother. You've gotta realise I know everything that goes on round here. You've got an orang-utan. Now, I don't know how you're keeping her hidden, and I don't care. I have two demands. Hey! Stop wobbling that stupid eye of yours and look at me! Now listen, you either comply with these two demands, or I'll tell your grandparents about the monkey. The guards too.'

CHAPTER SEVENTEEN: SOMETHING ELSE TO DO

She held up two fingers, in case he didn't know how many made two.

'Number one: your mates Sive and Dallan are going to play in the basketball match against Dundeer Dinesh at a time and place of my choosing. That jumped-up little guzzer needs to be put in his place. So they're gonna play, and we're gonna win. Or else.

'Number two: you're going to meet me tomorrow so I can take some pictures with the orang-utan to put up on Instagram. It'll be a savage post. I won't tell anyone how I met her – it'll just be me being gangsta with an ape. Nobody needs to know any more than that. You understand?'

'I don't know –'

'Save it, copper-top. Don't waste my time with your babbling. You know Wheelie Bin Alley, near the basketball court?'

'Yeah, 'course.'

'Bring her there for half three.' The gorgeous bully glared at him, her eyes cold and mean.

'Either I get some good pics or I blow your whole game wide open. You got me?'

'Yeah, I got you,' Onion muttered.

'Good. See you tomorrow. Wheelie Bin Alley. Don't be late or you'll be sorry.'

She turned around and strode off. Onion watched her go, then shook his head and closed the door. In the big scheme of things, he supposed, this was just one more ridiculous thing to do.

It wasn't like things could get any madder than they were already.

CHAPTER EIGHTEEN:
—
MISSION IMPROBABLE

The Five O's had a plan. They weren't sure it was a great plan, but none of them had ever tried to break an ape out of a circus before – this was all new territory for them.

The first problem was what to do with Róisín. They wanted to leave her in the attic, but they were afraid she might get upset and start making noise. Reluctantly, Onion agreed to leave Róisín in Molly's room. The pair had become good friends, and with Molly going to bed at eight o'clock, Granny probably wouldn't come into her room once she was settled. He turned the volume right down on Clíona's phone so it wouldn't make much noise. Onion told his granny that he would put Molly to bed that evening, which he did sometimes. He then explained the plan as simply as he could to his little sister, who promised to keep Róisín hidden if Granny came up. They could only hope that she did.

The second problem was that Onion and Derek were grounded. They bundled pillows and clothes into their beds to make it look like they were under the duvets, and then Clíona used Derek's phone to record them arguing and niggling at each other for about fifteen minutes. Putting this on a loop, she set it playing and, from outside the room, it sounded convincingly like the two brothers were stuck in the bedroom together. The brothers loudly said goodbye to the rest of the gang, ate their supper early and told their grandparents they were going to bed. Then they went upstairs to their room and set the phone playing the recording. Derek took two air horns from a box under his bed, then they crept back downstairs again, out the front door, softly closing it behind them, and hurried down the street to Dallan's house.

The third part of the plan was the diversion. Dallan had a large range of costumes: he put huge effort into Hallowe'en every year and dressing up as characters in school for World Book Day. He had two killer-clown costumes that he'd adapted into normal clown costumes by peeling off the blood.

He and Sive had made a banner too, which was already rolled up and tied to the crossbar of his bike. Dallan and Clíona put on the clown costumes and then they were ready to go.

Clíona's house was only a couple of doors down from the green where the circus was set up. If they could get Maya out, they'd bring Róisín's mother there by the back alley and hide her in the garden shed until they could find a better place for her.

The half-past six circus show was over and, as with the previous night, people were milling around chatting outside the Big Top. The sky was overcast and the light was fading, with a gloom settling over the tents and vehicles. People weren't happy. The Great Orangini had not appeared tonight. The circus had failed to produce its headline act. Some of the audience were asking for their money back.

'I'd say they were using Róisín as a hostage to get Maya to perform,' Derek guessed. 'Maya's probably refusing to do it now that they've lost her daughter.'

Part four of the plan: find Truck and steal the key to the chains. Onion, Sive and Derek wandered up, trying to act completely natural and not quite managing it. They slipped around the side of the Big Top, crawling under a caravan and coming out the other side near Truck's caravan, the one next to Maya's trailer.

Standing on tiptoes, Onion peeked in one of the windows. He saw the giant of a woman at a dressing table in full clown costume, retouching her make-up for the nine o'clock show. Her orange wig was on the table beside her, and beside that was a bunch of keys. The Five O's had figured she wouldn't carry her keys with her when she was doing her act, and they were right. Standing up, she left the keys on the table, put on her wig, nodded in satisfaction to herself and headed for the door. Onion and the others kept out of sight until she'd gone, then they crept around to the door and were relieved to find it unlocked. Derek sneaked inside while the others kept watch. Grabbing the keys, he jumped down the steps, closed the door and they darted back into hiding.

This was it. Time to make their move. Onion was sick with nerves, Sive was trembling and nearly choking on her gum and

Derek's face was a mask of tension, but they were ready.

Crouching behind a cage containing gas cylinders, Onion put his ear to the wall of Maya's trailer to see if he could hear her inside. He heard the clink of chains, which told him Maya was there, but he couldn't be sure she was alone. There was some rustling beside him, and he turned, putting a finger to his lips, shushing Sive. Sive, who wasn't making any noise, turned to Derek with her finger on her lips and shushed him. He was about to point out that he wasn't making any noise either, when he noticed the rustling behind him and turned to find Róisín sitting there, rubbing her hairy head against the mesh of the cage.

Derek jumped, giving the other two a fright, and both had to suppress yelps as they saw who was behind them.

'She can't stay here!' Onion hissed, his wonky eye starting to do spirals. 'How did she get out? We have to get her away or she's going to wreck everything. Maybe we should do this another night?'

'It's too late for that now – we've stolen the keys,' Sive said. 'It's now or never – we have to go for it. Send the signal!'

Onion took a heave on his inhaler. He nodded grimly and, with a shaky hand, he took the remote control from his pocket. He pressed the button and, away off in the distance, the church bell rang.

Chapter Nineteen:
The Diversion

Clíona and Dallan, all set in their clown costumes, heard the electronic bell ringing and got their bikes. Immediately, the people hanging around outside the Big Top started to comment and ask questions. Wasn't this a strange thing? What was happening to the church bell today? What was the world coming to? Would Father Murphy not get control of his bell, for goodness' sake?

'Let's do this thing!' Dallan said, his voice squeaky with nerves.

'Right on!' Clíona nodded and they did a fist bump.

CHAPTER NINETEEN: THE DIVERSION

Side by side on their bikes, they pulled apart so the banner unrolled between them. It was more than two metres wide. On it were the words 'SAY NO TO ANIMAL CRUELTY!' Clíona straightened the clown wig on her head, checked her red nose was firmly attached and nodded to her friend. Starting off a bit wobbly, they cycled out from the wall they were hiding behind and up the street towards the circus. The poles of the banner were taped to their saddles and each of them carried an air horn in their hands. They sped past the entrance to the circus, blasting their air horns and shouting, 'CLOWNS NOT CRUELTY! CLOWNS NOT CRUELTY!'

As a message, it wasn't very clear, but that wasn't the point. The main thing was to make a lot of noise so that Forester and his henchpeople would come out to see what all the fuss was about. The main thing was that Maya would be left alone for a few minutes.

'Dallan Okoye, what are you playing at?' a woman shouted as they cycled past.

'I'm not Dallan Okoye!' he shouted back. 'That's someone else.'

'Of course it's you, I'd know you anywhere!' the woman called to him. 'You came to my door in that outfit last Hallowe'en! What are you up to?'

'He's not Dallan!' Clíona repeated as they made an unsteady U-turn and headed back down the road.

'Don't you lie to me, Clíona O'Hare, or I'll be on to your mother!'

This wasn't going according to plan. They were supposed to keep their identities a secret. It was right then that the Garda car appeared at the top of the road. It was The Ferg and Garda Judge. The patrol car's roof lights flashed. In a panic, Dallan swerved right and Clíona swerved left and their banner tore in half, nearly pulling them off their bikes. They cycled off in different directions, neither knowing what to do next, each with half a banner flapping behind them. This wasn't how their diversion was supposed to go at all.

'Come on, Onion,' Dallan muttered. 'Hurry up, man. Hurry up!'

And then, from behind the Big Top, he heard the strangest sound. It was the frantic hooting of a mother ape who had just heard her daughter's voice.

CHAPTER TWENTY:

EVERYTHING GOES AS YOU'D EXPECT

Onion was hurrying up. He'd made it to the door of Maya's trailer and went to open it. It was locked. His hands were shaking so much he dropped Truck's keys twice.

Derek grabbed them from him and started trying one key after another in the lock. 'Come on, come on!' he was saying to himself through gritted teeth.

Sive was trying to keep Róisín calm. The ape was getting more and more wound up, jumping around and squealing. Inside, Maya had obviously heard her daughter's cries and started calling out with hoots, shaking her chains and thumping the floor and walls.

'Róisín, Róisín, you have to be quiet!' Onion pleaded with the young ape. 'Please! Everyone's going to hear us!'

It was too late. They heard the thumping of running footsteps behind them, and they spun around to see Truck coming at them, still in her clown gear but without her wig, her black hair flying free and fury on her face. Then a dark figure appeared on the roof of Forester's trailer. It was Bucket, dressed in his trapeze outfit, ready to leap down and pounce on them.

'RUN!' Onion shrieked.

So they ran. Róisín wouldn't leave her mother's door, so Derek grabbed her and carried her with him, but he wasn't going to get far hauling her weight.

'COME BACK WITH THAT APE, YA WEE PIGLETS!' Truck bellowed.

Bucket was silent. He leapt down from the roof in front of the three kids and their orangutan and would have caught them if a fourth kid

on a bike hadn't crashed into him
from behind, knocking
him over.

'WE NEED TO RUN AWAY NOW!'

Dallan wailed in terror, swinging his bike around, half of the torn banner hanging from the pole attached to his seat.

Clíona was pedalling across the green as fast as she could, the other half of the banner streaming out behind her, as a Garda car chased after her.

CHAPTER TWENTY: EVERYTHING GOES AS YOU'D EXPECT

Truck charged towards Onion and the others as Bucket bounded back onto his feet. Róisín squealed and tore free from Derek's grip, scampering under a caravan. There was no time to catch her. Bucket dropped down and went scrambling after her. The giant clown Truck kept coming for the kids, her face wrinkled up in a snarl.

The Five O's would have been caught right there and then if Maya hadn't started hammering her fists against the wall of her trailer, distracting the villains. Bucket came back out from under the trailer. He hadn't caught Róisín. Truck looked at him as he gestured urgently to her. They had to stop the mother ape making all that noise or people would start to suspect something. Bucket sprinted over to the door to try and calm the orang-utan down.

Those few seconds of distraction were enough for the gang to get out to the relative safety of the crowd, but they'd failed to help Maya and now they'd lost Róisín too. Forester was there, with some of the other performers around him. He was wearing a deeply suspicious expression. The rest of the Five O's watched as Clíona bounced across the grass on her bike and down the alley towards her house to escape from the patrol car, which skidded to a halt at the bollards that blocked the way.

The Ferg jumped out of the driver's seat, shouting after the cyclist, 'You come back here! Come back here right now! Impersonating a clown is a serious offence, and also takes a lot of skill and years of training. Years!'

'It's not a serious offence!' his partner snapped in disgust from the passenger seat of the car. 'It's not an offence at all. If it was, you'd be doing hard time, Fergus! Now will you get back in the car and stop embarrassing yourself.'

'It's still wrong!' The Ferg said with tears in his eyes. 'It's just wrong, Bridie. There has to be some justice in this world. You can't just throw on a costume and paint your face – you have to become the clown over time. That right there is an insult to the Clown Society and, believe me, those clowns take stuff like this very seriously.'

While this was going on, Dallan pulled off his red nose and wig, wiped at his make-up with his sleeve and, with a sad wave to the others, cycled off home. Sive hugged Onion and then she waved too and left. The O'Brien boys exchanged a look, keeping their faces turned away from Forester and his people, and headed off down their street.

Back at the house, they had to get in without their grandparents seeing them. Through the front window, they could see Granny and Grandad in the sitting-room, watching the news. Derek had taken the back-door key, so the boys made their way around the side of the house to the back garden. Derek was quietly unlocking the door when something grabbed Onion's thigh and he screamed like a parrot. It was Róisín, hugging his leg, looking desperately sad and shivering with fear. Onion picked her up and held her close. They all went inside and sneaked up the stairs.

They'd failed, completely and utterly. What were they going to do now?

Róisín wasn't happy about having to go back in the attic, but there was no way around it. They had to keep her out of sight. Derek tried taking Clíona's phone from her so she couldn't use it to make noise, only to have Róisín cling to it and bare her teeth, shaking her head furiously. In the end, they left her with it.

As they closed the attic hatch, the house phone rang and Granny came out to answer it. It was one of the neighbours, talking about some mad goings-on at the circus only a little while ago. Had she heard? Tongues would be wagging about this for some time, with Granny calling in to her husband about some of the best bits. It made everything seem so much worse.

Depressed and exhausted, the boys fell asleep. But their night was far from over.

CHAPTER TWENTY-ONE:
THE THING IN THE ATTIC

The noises were quiet at first. Gradually, however, they grew louder. Shuffles and thumps and scraping sounds. Squeaks and hoots. And then it started speaking.

'*I'm lonely,*' a distant, toneless voice said from somewhere up in the attic. '*Don't leave me alone. Somebody come and play with me.*'

Onion heard it and felt a sick feeling deep in his belly. He blinked and pulled on his glasses.

In the bed on the other side of the room, Derek was also awake. 'We are so dead,' he murmured.

'She found the volume button on the phone,' Onion moaned in dread.

'*I want my mammy. Please. I want my mammy.*'

Thump, thump, thump. Scrape. Thump, thump.

'Boys! Boys!' Granny's voice carried across the landing. 'Come out here right now!'

With heavy, reluctant steps, they trudged out of their room and over to their granny, who was standing in the open doorway of her own room. She seized them and hugged them tightly to her. From somewhere above them, they heard the faint voice: '*Come up and play with me. I'm lonely. Please play with me.*'

'Do you hear it, boys? Do you hear the voice from the other side?'

'The . . . other side?' Derek replied.

'Yes, I knew she'd come one day. I've been reading up on it,' said Granny.

'On what?' asked Onion.

Granny held up yet another ghost book she owned, The Other Side. 'It's my great-aunt Sarah trying to contact me,' Granny said as she looked towards the attic.

'I suppose . . . it could be your great-aunt,' Onion said, screwing his face up in a question to Derek, who shrugged in response. 'That's mad, isn't it?'

'Mad? It's terrifying, but I've read up on it so we'll be okay!' Granny exclaimed, letting go of her grandsons. 'Mairead down the road said the ghost of her uncle Harry was under the stairs. Well, now I have my own ghost. Take that, Mairead.'

'There's no such things as ghosts,' said Grandad Paddy.

'Then go up and check, Paddy!' Granny said in a very high-pitched voice. 'Why don't you go up and check the attic if there's no such thing as ghosts? But I bet you'll come face to face with my great-aunt Sarah,' said Granny in a hypnotic voice.

Grandad didn't reply for a few seconds, but he didn't look too happy about going up in the attic. Then he growled, rolled his eyes and pushed past Granny to reach for the pole to pull down the hatch.

'Paddy! What are you doing?' Granny cried.

'What do you think I'm doing, Mary? I'm looking up in the attic, like you said.'

'Here, take these.' Granny grabbed a tin of biscuits from the hot press. So that's where she stashes the fancy Christmas biscuits, thought Onion. It's no wonder they were always half-melted.

'Great-Aunt Sarah loved a bikky. Paddy is coming up with a bikky for ya, Sarah!' Granny roared as she placed a chocolate digestive in the top pocket of Grandad's shirt. 'If she comes at you, throw the biscuit in the corner of the attic. She'll follow that so you can escape, Paddy.'

CHAPTER TWENTY-ONE: THE THING IN THE ATTIC

'What in the name of God?' Grandad was looking tough, but his face had gone very pale. He glanced anxiously towards the hatch.

'To be honest, Paddy, I think we need to call Father Murphy. We might need a professional to exorcise Great-Aunt Sarah out of the attic,' said Granny.

Grandad scowled. 'You want to call the priest? In the middle of the night? To come over to check our attic? For a ghost? And what will he make of that, do ya think, Mary? What will the neighbours think?'

This threw a new light on things. Granny wouldn't want the neighbours knowing about this before she had the chance to tell them herself. And Father Murphy was an awful gossip.

'Let me look in the blinkin' attic and then at least we'll know if we have a ghost or not,' Grandad said. 'Then you can dial 999 for the priest. How's that?'

Granny nodded fearfully and gave a loud gulp. Onion was feeling very guilty about scaring his granny now, yet part of him was still hoping that somehow this would all go away. He had no idea why he still had notions like this because, in his experience, no serious problem in his life ever just 'went away', but he still held out hope that, some day, one would. Maybe today was that day.

'All right then, a quick look,' Granny said. 'But you stay on that ladder!'

Onion and Derek watched, resigned to their doom, as their grandfather pulled down the hatch.

'That's a much smoother action on those hinges,' he said. 'It's like they've been oiled.'

'Sarah! Great-Aunt Sarah! Paddy is coming up but there's no need to fear him. He has a bikky in his pocket for ya,' said Granny in a weird ghostly voice.

'Would you stop it, Mary? The chocolate biscuit is melting in me pocket. I want to get this over and done with,' said Grandad, scowling.

CHAPTER TWENTY-ONE: THE THING IN THE ATTIC

He was looking pretty nervous himself. He licked his lips, blessed himself (Grandad never blessed himself) and slowly climbed up the ladder. Taking a deep breath, as if there might be poison gas or some such up there, he stuck his head up through the hatch quickly, looked left, looked right and then clambered back down the ladder, folded it up and slammed the hatch closed.

'Nothing! All fine!' he declared. 'Everyone go back to bed.'

'*Nobody will play with me!*' the voice whined. '*I'm lonely. I want my mammy.*'

'Your mother is dead a long time, Sarah. Sorry, love,' shouted Granny.

'Must be a radio left on next door,' Grandad assured them, walking past everyone and into his bedroom. 'There's nothing in the attic, I had a good old look now. Let's all go back to bed and let the priest have a root around tomorrow, eh?'

'She must have gone back to the other side,' explained Granny.

'Róisín must have been hiding behind a box or something,' Onion whispered to his brother. 'Probably got a fright when she heard Grandad coming.'

Granny kissed each of her grandsons on their heads, pushed them into their room, wished them goodnight, told them to say their prayers, especially for Great-Aunt Sarah, and closed the door. A few seconds later, her bedroom door closed too. The two brothers lay awake in the darkness, both of them staring at the ceiling.

'So . . .' Derek said at last. 'Now Father Murphy's going to come over and check our attic for ghosts. Onion, man – this is really starting to get out of hand.'

CHAPTER TWENTY-TWO:
THE FIVE O'S IN DISGUISE

O nion rang the church bell again to call an emergency meeting with the Five O's before school. All of the neighbours went in and out of their doors like cuckoos from a cuckoo clock, bobbing up and down and blessing themselves, not sure if they should go to Mass or to work. Father Murphy just stood in his driveway looking up at the bell with his arms folded, nodding to himself as if it had finally broken him.

As usual when things had to be kept quiet, the Five O's met in Onion's bedroom. The rest of the gang were delighted to hear that Róisín had come back. But what with the failed break-out attempt and Granny calling the parish priest about the 'ghost' in the attic, some of them felt it was time to question whether bringing two orang-utans to live in a housing estate in Ballinlud was such a good idea. It was getting very hard to keep a lid on things. Onion was insistent that they should see this through, and Sive and Dallan were still supporting him, though they were having doubts. Derek thought they should look for another home for the apes, and Clíona was torn between having their own personal orang-utans and the practicalities of looking after a pair of large primates.

'Oh, I forgot to mention it yesterday,' Onion said, grinning nervously. 'We have to take Róisín to Wheelie Bin Alley after school today. Tina Dalton knows we have her, and she wants to take photos to put on Instagram. If we don't, she's going to tell everyone we have an ape, starting with Granny and Grandad.'

'Aw, what?' Derek burst out. 'You're only telling us this NOW?'

'I kind of forgot because of the whole escape-plan thing,' Onion said, shrugging. 'It got pushed out of my head. Oh, and she has another condition too. Sive and Dallan have to play in her basketball match against Dundeer Dinesh's team.'

'What?' Sive snapped, nearly choking on her chewing gum. 'No way! No way am I playing for that evil cow!'

'Yeah, no way!' Dallan agreed, folding his arms.

'If we don't agree to her terms, she tells everyone,' Onion said again. 'We don't have any choice. She'll blow the whistle on us, and I'm honestly not sure where Róisín would end up or how many laws we've broken by now. If The Ferg is right, we broke another one last night by impersonating clowns.'

'I really don't think it's against the law to impersonate a clown,' Derek said. 'Too many people do it. But no more messing with the guards, okay? If Granny and Grandad find out half of what we've done, me and Onion will be old and grey before they let us out again. We'll be like those shrivelled old guys who don't want to leave prison because they've been locked up so long they're afraid of the outside world.'

'He's not joking,' Onion said, shuddering.

'We should find someone who can help,' Clíona suggested again. 'Someone who knows about orang-utans. We don't know what we're doing! I think we should contact Doctor and Major Michaels, those primatologists from the wildlife park. We just don't tell them about Róisín, that's all.'

'First things first,' Sive spoke up. 'If Father Murphy is coming to get the ghost out of your attic, then we have to hide Róisín somewhere else.'

'I've told Mam I need to stay home today,' Clíona said. 'She'll be at work, so I'll take Róisín home with me and look after her there.'

CHAPTER TWENTY-TWO: THE FIVE O'S IN DISGUISE

Clíona's mam, Vlasta O'Hare, was not like most parents. She treated Clíona like she was almost an adult and let her do things that most other parents wouldn't, like read grown-up books, work with explosive chemicals or just stay at home if Clíona asked, because she assumed her daughter would spend the time well.

When the teachers had complained that that wasn't how school was supposed to work, Vlasta had pointed out that Clíona had been bullied by classmates for nearly two years and that wasn't how school was supposed to work either. She informed them that if the staff wanted to start taking her daughter's education as seriously as Vlasta did, Clíona would start taking her attendance seriously too.

Clíona's mam was hard core.

'I'll pull a sickie at lunchtime and come back and help out,' Sive said. 'I'll tell the teachers I have an earache.'

Unlike Vlasta O'Hare, Sive's parents took attendance and grades very seriously, but they knew she did too. Though she might not have been as smart as Clíona, she hardly missed a day. Her parents would fall for a sickie every now and then. The teachers were never really sure how Sive's hearing aids worked, so an earache was always a good excuse. She'd feel guilty about it . . . but not that guilty.

'There's something else,' Clíona said. 'I found this online when I got home last night.'

Clíona had brought her tablet with her. Because it had no phone connection, she had saved the photo she'd found on a news site. It was a blurred picture of Róisín running along the street. In the background, a sign was just visible on the wall: 'Ballinlud Avenue' – the main road that ran past the green where the circus was set up. The headline read 'Sighting of Mysterious Ape in Ballinlud'.

CHAPTER TWENTY-TWO: THE FIVE O'S IN DISGUISE

'Some kid took this last night and posted it online,' Clíona told them. 'By now, half of Ireland's going to know there's an orang-utan loose out here.'

'Oh, this is great!' Derek said with a snort.

'How are we going to get her over to Clíona's house?' Sive asked, chomping hard on her gum. 'We'll have to walk her down the street in broad daylight. We'll have to carry her in something, covered up. Should we try to borrow a shopping trolley or . . . anybody any ideas?'

'We're going to dress up,' Dallan told them. He'd been unusually quiet, as if he'd been waiting for this moment. He had a sports bag with him, and now he unzipped it. 'We're going to disguise her with this.'

He'd brought another one of his costumes. It was a gorilla suit. The other four kids stared at the suit, and then at him, and then back at the suit.

'You . . . you want to walk the orang-utan down the street by disguising her as . . . as a gorilla?' Sive asked in a flat voice.

'No,' Dallan replied, glaring back at her. 'I want to disguise the orang-utan as a person wearing a gorilla suit. Then the rest of us will put on some costumes too, so it looks like we're all off to a costume event somewhere. We only have to wear them between here and Clíona's house.'

There was a very long pause as everyone thought about this.

'That's so stupid it might actually work,' Derek admitted.

And that was what they did. Grandad had already headed out on a job, so while Onion and Derek went downstairs to distract Granny by asking her about ghosts, Dallan, Sive and Clíona brought Róisín down from the attic and attempted to get her into the gorilla costume. It was one of Dallan's old ones, too small for him now, but it was still very baggy on Róisín. The legs were too long and the arms were too short. It didn't help that Molly was up by this point and was having fits of giggles watching them try to convince an ape to disguise herself as another ape. Róisín was happy to dump the ballerina dress and blue bows, but she did not want to get into the costume. As the three kids managed to get her into one part of it, she'd wriggle out of another. Eventually, they had to keep her busy with fruit as they dressed her and finally, finally persuaded her to put on the mask, which she absolutely hated.

'We are going to be so late for school,' Derek grumbled as the group left the house. To add to his bad mood, Onion was dressed as a cowboy, Sive as a witch, Clíona as a giant lizard and Dallan as a vampire, and Derek was cloaked in embarrassment. He walked ahead of them to try and keep his humiliation to a minimum, but other teenagers on their walk to school spotted them and laughed, jeering and cracking jokes.

'Everyone thinks we're eejits,' Sive moaned.

'Everyone thinks we're eejits anyway,' Onion reminded her. 'This is nothing new. Róisín, leave the mask alone – I can see your chin!'

It was only a couple of minutes to Clíona's house, and her mother had already gone to work. Derek kept walking, catching up with some of his mates from school and throwing his hands up in disgust at what his little brother got up to with

his stupid gang. And though it might all have looked daft, it worked. Even with all the children and teenagers heading along the road to school, nobody noticed that the person dressed in the gorilla costume was an orang-utan.

Once they were safely in Clíona's house, everyone pulled off their costumes to reveal their school uniforms. Onion, Dallan and Sive hugged Róisín, wished Clíona good luck and then headed

out to school. On the way, they passed the circus. A big khaki-coloured SUV was parked on the road in front of it, with a logo of leafy letters on the side: 'Tota Freedom Wildlife Park'. A man and woman were standing beside the truck, looking from the Big Top over to the sign for Ballinlud Avenue on the other side of the road.

They were slightly scruffy, outdoorsy types in outdoorsy clothes with lots of pockets. They had weathered faces, bad haircuts and wore hiking boots. They were staring at the spot where Róisín had been photographed the previous night. Onion nudged Dallan, recognising the couple from another picture Clíona had shown them. They were the primatologists, Doctor Michelle Michaels and Major Mike Michaels.

They'd come searching for the Ape of Ballinlud.

CHAPTER TWENTY-THREE:
RÓISÍN'S NEW LOOK

The school day seemed to take for ever. When they eventually got out, Onion and Dallan made straight for Clíona's house. They didn't have much time if they were going to get down to Wheelie Bin Alley for half-past three to meet Tina. Neither boy was feeling good about this. The gorilla costume had worked once, distracting people for a couple of minutes along the road, but the alley was a ten-minute walk away, most of it along the main road. And now a pair of ape experts were in the area, looking for an orang-utan. There was no way they'd be fooled if they spotted Róisín in that costume.

Fortunately, Clíona and Sive had been working on this problem through the day. When the boys arrived, they found Róisín already dressed and ready to go. Instead of the gorilla costume, she was wearing black trousers, a black button-up jacket with fancy buttons and a high collar, a pair of big dark sunglasses and a wig of long black hair that hung over her face. A coat of foundation had made her skin less grey, though only a little bit was showing. The high collar on the jacket helped hide the red hair under her chin, and white fringes on the cuffs meant only the tips of her fingers were showing. A pair of soft slip-on runners concealed her hand-like feet. The phone on the cord around her neck completed the look. She gave the boys a cheeky grin.

'This is cool!' Onion said, genuinely impressed.

'She's a goth,' Sive told him. 'We've even taught her how to avoid speaking. Try asking her question.'

'Hey there, stranger,' Dallan said. 'What's your name?'

CHAPTER TWENTY-THREE: RÓISÍN'S NEW LOOK

Róisín snorted, stared at the screen of her phone, said 'Tch' and gave a little toss of her head, as if answering such a question was beneath her dignity.

'That's exactly like Derek,' Onion said in wonder. 'You've trained an ape to be a teenager!'

'It wasn't as hard as you'd think,' Sive said modestly. 'They've a lot in common.'

'And she's a teenage goth,' Clíona added. 'She has to play the part – mope around, keep her head down. She's short and she still doesn't look right when she walks, but as long as we stay crowded around her, she won't stand out too much when we're on the road.'

'This is genius,' Dallan said. 'Róisín, you are rockin' that look!'

Róisín said 'Tch' and snorted.

It was time to go. They wished Derek was coming with them – they could have done with the older boy on their side when they met Tina and her thugs – but he didn't get out of school until four. He was going to meet them in Wheelie Bin Alley, assuming they were still there and nothing had gone wrong. For some reason, they all felt like something was going to go wrong. Perhaps it had to do with the fact that only a complete fool would trust Tina Dalton. Yet they had no choice.

CHAPTER TWENTY-FOUR:
—
THE AMBUSH

Tina was waiting at the top of the alley with the Bang-Off-Them Brothers, trying not to look at the white van parked a few metres down from the mouth of the lane, in front of the flower shop. Forester was waiting in that van, with his oddly silent trapeze artist and the huge powerlifting clown. The plan was to draw Onion O'Brien's losers round the corner of the alley, out of sight of the road, and then act all surprised when Forester and his henchpeople came round and cornered them. She wanted to nail this operation. Forester was a proper villain, and there was a lot she could learn from him.

Top 5 Reasons
Why Tina Is Pure Evil

1. Giving lemons to babies and telling them they're sweets, making the babies' faces turn inside out with the bitterness

2. Stealing fifty quid from her father's wallet (crime, like charity, begins at home)

3. Laughing and pointing at random people to make them paranoid

4. Setting fire to Larry's schoolbag with dog poo inside it, so that when Larry stood on the bag to put the fire out, dog poo went everywhere

5. Stealing ten quid from her mother's purse (a trial run for the fifty-quid heist)

Wheelie Bin Alley ran behind an arcade of shops, down past the two schools and the leisure centre. Its name came from the bins that lined the alley and which were useful for climbing over the wall behind the shops and into the weed-infested basketball court beyond. The court was part of a large neglected common area used by people in Ballinlud, and so the alley was used as a shortcut to the shops and the bus stop for routes into the city.

Tina saw the Five O's gang coming down the road towards her. She allowed herself a sly little smile before slipping into the alley, confident they'd follow her in. Barry and Larry were with her, as ever – loyal boys, even though they had the personality of a toilet seat. Then Onion came into the alley, but where was the ape? Tina made an 'Oh' expression with her pretty face. There! The short little goth in the middle of the group! Tina nearly laughed out loud. There they were with an orang-utan right out on the street and nobody could see it. That was pretty clever. Maybe she should give these losers a place in her gang. She could call on a crew of about a dozen or so, but she didn't actually like many of them. And the Five O's might offer more interesting conversation than the two planks behind her.

All that could come later. Any second now, Forester was going to make his move.

'Hey, Dalton! The time has come to draw a circle and put a name in it!'

No, she thought. Not now. Not now! Turning to look up, she saw Dundeer Dinesh and four of his gang on top of the wall to her right. They were wearing sunglasses and had jewellery draped over their American basketball vests. Dinesh was tall, dark and gangly and was looking mean.

'I've waited long enough,' he said. 'Either we play this game now or you hand over your territory, like a dog in a basket. What's it going to be: the territory or the name in a circle?'

Everyone looked confused, even Dinesh's gang. He was always talking in riddles.

He thought it made him seem mysterious and intelligent. It didn't.

'How did you know I was here?' she demanded.

'Barry told me,' Dinesh replied, pointing at her henchman.

Tina turned on Barry, thumping him in the ribs. 'Why did you do that?' she barked at him.

'Because he asked?' Barry said, only now realising it might have been a bad thing to do. He got another thump to confirm it.

It had been two weeks since Dinesh had challenged her to the match. She didn't have Forester's money yet to hire the star players from Tallum, and she couldn't get that money without the ape. Sive and Dallan were just her back-up plan, but she might have to use them yet.

'I'm not ready,' she said. 'My squad has injuries. I need more time.'

'You've had time. Now time has arrived, and waiting for more time is just a pipe dream,' he grunted. 'Are you ready to play or not? I'm the daddy and I'm gonna prove it like DNA!'

Tina sighed. Dinesh figured himself for a gangsta rapper, though he didn't actually rap. There was no denying he was a serious threat, though. He was king of the primary school kids in Dundeer, and he swore that he'd put his heel on Ballinlud next. Over Tina's dead body. Or better yet, his.

The Five O's were standing behind her now, trying to figure out what was going on.

She pointed at Sive and Dallan. 'You're up,' she said. 'We're playing and we're going to win. Or you know what will happen.'

She saw Bucket peer around the corner of the alley. They couldn't spring their trap now. Too many witnesses. She cursed under her breath. And the ape was right here! If anyone saw the animal now, she'd never get her money.

'Niall, call in the crowd,' Dinesh said to one of his gang.

CHAPTER TWENTY-FOUR: THE AMBUSH

With a big movement to make sure everyone saw, Niall, a slightly shorter, paler version of Dinesh, pulled out a phone and dialled a number. It was a short call. 'It's on,' he said simply and hung up. To Dinesh, he added, 'They're coming.'

Tina led the Five O's up onto the bins, over the wall and down onto the old tarmac of the basketball court. The court was in bad shape, the paint peeling on the backboards, the remains of the netting hanging loosely from the hoops, rust setting into the metalwork. She faced Dinesh and he flipped a coin, slapped it down on his hand and let her call it. She picked tails, won the toss and chose her end of the court. Sive and Dallan reluctantly walked over to stand with the Bang-Off-Them Brothers to make up Tina's team of five, while Dinesh's gang faced off against them.

And then, with a rumble of feet, dozens of other kids came over the wall and running across the field and appeared from behind nearby buildings. Word had got out about the grudge match. Everyone was coming to see this game.

Tina saw Onion and Clíona shuffle in front of the goth orang-utan, trying to block her from everyone's sight, and she cursed again. All her carefully laid plans were going down the toilet. Dinesh was going to pay for this. He was going to pay big time. First, though, she had to win this game, and if this pair from the Five O's didn't do their bit, she'd make the rest of their lives a misery.

CHAPTER TWENTY-FIVE:
—
PLAYING DIRTY

Onion didn't play much basketball, on account of his asthma, his eye patch, his stick-thin limbs and being generally rubbish at sports. He was always the last to be picked for teams, and there were only five players on a basketball team, so normally a lot of other people would get picked before a team captain was desperate enough to let Onion play. He understood the rules well enough to follow the game because he'd spent hours standing on sidelines. He wondered what Róisín would make of all this and hoped she wouldn't get bored and start doing ape stuff that would attract unwanted attention.

It was a rough game from the start and nobody expected it to be any different. Dinesh's team, four boys and a girl, were skilled and mean and didn't take the rules very seriously. Not that Tina and the twins did either. In a matter of seconds, Dinesh's side had battered their way down to Tina's end and their leader planted a perfect shot into the hoop, leaving Sive to catch it as it fell. Sive immediately made her run forward, dribbling the ball around Dinesh before passing to Barry, who bounced it to Tina, who dodged past two more of the Dundeer gang to even the score with a lay-up.

There was as much pushing and shoving as there was dribbling and passing, with everyone picking up bruises, grazes and scrapes from their falls onto the tarmac. The twin brothers were good at getting in their opponents' way, but they were slow on their feet. Sive and Dallan were doing all the running around and it was wearing them down. Dallan scored an arcing shot from the three-point mark to put Ballinlud in front and got charged from behind, the blow to his back sending him sprawling to the ground. He got up, snarled at his attacker and anxiously checked his glasses weren't broken. Unlike Onion's chunky value-brand spectacles, Dallan's glasses were expensive designer frames. His parents would have a fit if something happened to them.

The pace of the game did not let up. Onion could feel Róisín close behind him, peering around, watching the game from under his arm, fascinated by what was going on. Dinesh's team were dirty players, but they were good too and they were pulling ahead. It was thirty-six twenty-five to Dundeer and they were playing first to fifty. The ball pounded the ground, bodies thudded and breaths came fast and shallow.

Then Larry went to block a pass from Dinesh and got it badly wrong. Instead of catching the ball in his hands, it smacked him full in the face. It knocked him clean out, and he fell on his back. The others were scared at first, thinking they might have to call some grown-ups, until Barry assured them that Larry took a lot of hits on the head and he'd be okay. The game could go on.

Ballinlud were one man short and well behind. Tina was raging; Dallan and Sive were exhausted. None of them was playing well now. Onion could see how this was going to go. They'd lose and Tina would turn nasty and want revenge, and then she'd probably tell the whole world about Róisín. Everything was about to come apart.

The ball bounced over the line and rolled to his feet. Before he could pick it up and throw it to Tina, who was coming over for it, Róisín picked it up. She started bouncing it. Stepping up to the line, she threw it to Sive, signing for her human friend to pass it back to her.

And then everything changed.

Trusting her instincts, Sive passed the ball back to the orang-utan in disguise, and Róisín moved like she was born for the basketball court. Left, right, she dodged past one Dundeer guy, then another, bounced the ball through the legs of a third, ducked under Dinesh's grasping hands, ran up the back of the fifth opponent and leapt . . . grabbing the hoop and dumping the ball down through it. The crowd burst into cheers.

In the following few minutes, Ballinlud destroyed the Dundeer players. Róisín needed someone to pass to from time to time, but mostly she was like a whirlwind. Shorter than everyone else, her arms were still longer, and she was faster and more agile, the ball spinning and hammering in her hands, a blur the others couldn't keep up with. In the end, she flew into the air to slam the ball through the basket for the fiftieth point and dropped to the ground to a thunder of applause from the sidelines. Nobody had ever seen a match like this.

'Who is that girl?' a boy next to Onion asked. 'She's a bit, like, funny-shaped, but I think I'm in love.'

'She's the daughter of The Great Orangini!' Onion replied, overcome with emotion.

It was only then that he saw Róisín had lost one of her shoes in the last jump up to the hoop. People would see her hand-shaped foot. He looked over to her in alarm, only to have his view blocked as the crowd rushed in to congratulate her. He saw her snort with disdain and toss her head in response to their praise. Tina grabbed the shoe and pushed through the press of bodies to try and reach the ape, holding the shoe with awe, like that prince who gets dumped at the ball by Cinderella.

Róisín turned her gaze to Onion, and then her face, still mostly covered by sunglasses and long black hair, was struck with an expression of terror. Onion swivelled to glance behind him and saw Forester, the ringmaster, standing at the end of the court. Róisín gave a shriek and scrambled through the crowd, raced for the wall by the alley and bounded over it, disappearing from sight. Onion called after her, rushing to follow her. She'd panicked and left her friends and now she was all alone and on the run.

Which, of course, was exactly what the ringmaster wanted.

CHAPTER TWENTY-SIX:
—
GIVING CHASE

In all the chaos of the crowd, Sive, Dallan and Clíona missed Róisín going over the wall. It was only when they saw Onion clambering over in his usual gangle of limbs that they realised something must be up. People were standing around, congratulating the Ballinlud players, saying they were legends and wasn't that little goth one a real find. Clíona was waving frantically to the other two, but it took a minute for them to get free.

By that time, Róisín and Onion had both vanished round the corner and out the end of the alley, and there were three different directions they could have gone from there: right or left up the main road, or into the estate directly across from the mouth of the alley. They were at a loss at first, until they saw a nearby white van pulling away from the arcade of shops. Bucket was at the wheel, and Forester was sitting beside him.

'They must have kidnapped them!' Dallan cried. 'What are we going to do?'

'We're going to kidnap them back!' Sive declared, running after the van and banging on the side of it.

Then the van drove off and left her standing in the road.

'When we get to the circus, we'll kidnap them back!' she added.

An SUV stopped behind her and she jumped onto the path, waving an apology to the driver. It drew alongside, a khaki-coloured four-wheel drive with 'Tota Freedom Wildlife Park' printed along the side in safari-style lettering. There was an outdoorsy couple sitting in the front seats. The window on their side opened and Derek stuck his head out.

'Oi, get in, you lot!' he called to them.

'We've had this all wrong! Róisín and her mam don't belong to the circus. They never did. Get in, we're going after them!'

The three kids piled in beside him, and he introduced the man and woman as the door slammed shut.

'This is Doctor Michelle Michaels and Major Mike Michaels – they run Tota Freedom Wildlife Park.'

'I know!' Clíona retorted. 'I was the one who told you who they were. I've been talking about them the whole time. You all told me I wasn't to say anything to them. So why are we in their car?'

'Hi, Clíona,' Michelle said as her husband set off after Forester's van. 'And you must be Dallan and Sive. Pleased to meet you.'

She was in her fifties and had a lively face with dark skin lined by the sun, sharp brown eyes and a smiley mouth. Her hair looked like she cut it herself with blunt scissors and no mirror.

'Let me explain. Derek saw us outside the circus and started asking questions about orang-utans. He really was trying not to be obvious about it, but we figured out he knew something about Maya and her child.

'You see, Maya was stolen from us a few years ago. She was born in our wildlife park. There aren't many of these lovely apes left, and we're trying to help them breed. The visitors loved her – she was so playful and a real acrobat. A proper show-off! We didn't put it together at the time, but Forester's circus was set up nearby, and they left just after she disappeared. Forester stole her from us and took to the road. She was pregnant when she was taken, which is how they ended up with Róisín too.

'When we saw the picture online of an orang-utan who'd be the right age to be Maya's child, we came over as quickly as we could. And here was Forester and his circus again, after all this time. Derek has told us the secret of "The Great

Orangini". I can assure you, you've done nothing wrong. Mister Joe Forester and his circus stole a highly intelligent, endangered animal, chained her up, trained her to perform dangerous tricks to make themselves rich and kept her child hostage to make her behave. They've broken the law and they're going to pay for it.'

'What are you going to do?' Dallan asked.

'Do?' Major Mike Michaels asked, his thickly bearded face looking in the mirror at the kids in the back seat. 'We have informed the necessary people in charge, or "the guards" as they are commonly known, and we're going to see that Forester is carted off to prison like the fiend he is. That's what you do with someone who steals an orang-utan.'

'Oh, right,' Dallan said, wincing. 'Maybe we should just have done that at the start then.'

'We thought we might be able to keep them,' Sive explained. 'We didn't know they were yours.'

Mike laughed, and it was a nice sound. 'I'd have done exactly the same thing when I was your age!' he said, grinning at his wife. 'Now let's go get these ape-nappers, shall we?'

'Man, Onion's going to be really upset when he finds out he can't keep Róisín,' Clíona said softly. 'He really had his heart set on it.'

'I don't mean to be a bit of a downer,' Derek said. 'But Forester must know you're onto him now. And to prove he's committed a crime, you have to catch him with the apes, right? If I was him, I'd be trying to get rid of them as soon as I can. He'll want to make sure they disappear for ever. And if Onion's with Róisín, he's going to mess all that up. Believe me, messing things up is what Onion does best. He's spectacular at it. So tell me this: how nasty do you think Forester is, and what would he do to someone who gets in his way?'

The Michaels glanced at each other, and then the major hit the accelerator.

CHAPTER TWENTY-SEVEN:
APE ON THE RUN

Onion was messing this up, he knew it. Róisín didn't run down the alley as he'd expected. She'd scampered straight in through the back door of a shop. Onion followed her in, finding himself in the kitchen of a Chinese takeaway. His stomach rumbled as he rushed through a thick fog of rich smells, trying to keep up with the frightened ape, angry shouts ringing in his ears from the men and women working there.

Róisín barrelled through, kicking off her other shoe and pulling off her wig, sunglasses and clothes as she scooted along, leaving a trail of discarded items behind her. Now the only thing

she was wearing was Clíona's phone on the cord around her neck, which was still overdressed for an orang-utan.

She took the feet out from under a man who was standing with a wok in his hand, the food flying everywhere. He pulled a table over as he fell, and pots and utensils crashed to the tiled floor. A woman with a deep Cavan accent shouted curses at the intruders. Out at the serving counter, a teenage girl studying the menu screamed when a mad-looking red-haired ape pounced on the counter in front of her, let out a screech and dived past her.

This run through the restaurant must have caught Forester's lot by surprise because they were nowhere in sight when Onion ducked under the hatch in the counter and emerged through the front door after Róisín.

Then he spotted Bucket, who was standing just inside the mouth of the alley, obviously waiting for them to appear there. He had a catch pole, the kind of metal pole with a loop on the end used for nabbing stray dogs. His attention was so set on what might come out of the alley, he didn't see Róisín when she bounded across the road in front of a double-decker bus, the driver sounding his horn angrily.

Onion was still giving chase, though his lungs were already burning, his breathing getting increasingly gaspy. He wasn't built for pursuit. He heard Forester bellowing something from the alley and knew the villains were coming across the road after him now. Róisín did a hard turn left, ran down the footpath along a line of parked cars, then seemed to panic, not knowing what to do. She came racing back past Onion again, swerved right, out behind a car and . . . jumped into the bus as it was about to close its doors. Not knowing what else to do, Onion staggered up and lurched on after her.

'Two please,' he wheezed and dropped the coins into the ticket machine as the bus pulled away.

The driver looked like he might object, though maybe he wasn't sure what the rules were about orang-utans on a bus. Still, though, this was Dublin and weren't there all sorts of strange characters around? The man shrugged and printed out the two tickets. Róisín hugged Onion's legs, trembling violently. Shuffling forward with the ape on his leg, he sat down on the nearest free seat, picked her up and hugged her. Everyone was looking at them. And sure, why wouldn't they?

Onion was heaving in breaths, his lungs trying to catch up with his pounding heart. Róisín was clutching him, her gaze glassy as she stared out the window. The bus took them up Ballinlud Avenue. The second stop was next to the circus. Onion was just getting his breath back when Róisín lifted her head, hooted urgently and dropped from his lap as the back doors opened.

'Aw no,' he groaned. 'Róisín, please . . . no.'

But she was already gone, out onto the path and scooting over the grass towards the caravans and trailers. Onion grunted and hurried off the bus to follow her. The Big Top was being taken down, men taking the fabric around the sides out first, as others loosened the ropes on the huge sheet that hung from the four centre poles. It was a tough task, and none of them noticed the little ape who passed them, finding her way to her mother's trailer.

She began pulling hopelessly at the locked door, then signed to Onion, the phone translating:

'LET ME IN! OPEN THE DOOR! I WANT MY MAMMY! I WANT MY MAMMY!'

She scrabbled at the door again. Onion jogged up behind her and watched her. She was desperate to get to her mother, who had heard her and was calling out from inside, shaking her chains. Some of the circus workers were looking over now. They'd spotted the orang-utan.

'Róisín, please, we can't stay here,' he started to say, wanting to cry himself when he saw how upset she was. 'Please, girl. I'm just a kid – I can't hold them off. They'll catch you and take you back! We can't—'

Then he put his hands in his pockets. He felt the bunch of keys that he'd kept because he didn't know what to do with them. Truck's keys. A couple of guys were climbing down from the Big Top now. Others, on the ground, were looking in his direction. Onion gulped. Every instinct was telling him to run. He wasn't cut out for this.

There'd be no hiding if he did this, no keeping it a secret. No hope of keeping Róisín. Hardly aware of what he was doing, he took the keys from his pocket, tried a couple to find the right one and unlocked the door. He opened it and Róisín scrambled inside to her mother. The two apes hooted and cried with joy as they embraced. Onion saw a man drop to the ground beside the tent and start striding towards the trailer.

In seconds, Onion was inside, finding the keyholes in Maya's shackles and fumbling with the keys. Seeing that he was trying to help, she held still until he'd unlocked her, then she gathered Róisín in her arms and ran to the door. The man from the Big Top was just coming up to the steps and Maya leapt out, her feet hitting him in the chest, throwing him backwards, and then she was away, galloping across the grass on all fours, with Róisín riding piggyback.

Onion took off after them and saw Maya making for the road. As she was passing the Big

Top, a white van swerved off the road, up over the kerb and onto the grass. Truck and Bucket jumped out, both holding catch poles, their loops ready to snatch at Maya's neck.

The orang-utan swung around, then ran back in the other direction. As she passed Onion, she picked him up and threw him over her shoulder. He was pretty tall for his age, but there wasn't much meat on his stick-thin body. She carried him as if he was nothing but a doll, rushing into the Big Top, making for the far side and the open area of grass beyond it. Other circus workers appeared in a line in front of her, as if trying to herd her back.

Maya turned again, and this time she headed for one of the ladder-like centre poles that held up the huge main sheet of the massive tent.

'Oh no, wait, hang on . . .' Onion panted as his belly bounced painfully on her shoulder. 'Maya, wait. I really don't want to—'

And then, with one bound, she was climbing. She didn't climb like some kid clambering up a tree, bit by bit, she swung up with effortless speed, even though she was carrying two other bodies. Rising a metre or more at a time, each lunge or jump brought her long arms up to catch hold again, swinging from side to side as she rushed upwards as easily as Onion could run along a path. He wheezed in terror, his head hanging upside down and the world around swaying from side to side, his view getting gradually wider as they sped up the centre pole. He desperately wanted to take a puff of his inhaler, which was dangling around his forehead and banging against his face, but he had his arms around Maya's waist and was too petrified to let go.

CHAPTER TWENTY-SEVEN: APE ON THE RUN

Up they went, up through the hole in the top of the tent, right up to the top of the pole. It was strung with cables to support the structure, and a latticed metal beam joined it to a second pole several metres away. The whole of Ballinlud stretched out around him, upside down, and he felt sickeningly dizzy. Onion didn't know how high up he was, but he was sure that if he fell from here, he'd have plenty of time to know he was about to die before he actually died, which was almost scarier than the thought of dying itself.

'Please, Maya! LET ME DOWN!' he wailed, his stomach clenching with every movement. 'Please, please, can we go down? I don't want to die! Or be really badly hurt! Or even be a little bit hurt! Can we just stop moving for a second? Can you stay still? Ow! You're holding on really tight – aaagggh! No, DO hold on tight! DON'T LET GO! Please, can we go down?! PLEASE!'

Then, with his upside-down view, he saw Truck climbing up the ladder-like pole below him, fury written on her face.

'This is the end of the show, Maya!' she snarled. 'The Great Orangini is gonna take a bad wee fall, pet!'

Maya was panting with effort now, feeling the weight of her load. She bared her teeth at the woman, grunted angrily at her and made a very rude gesture that you didn't need sign language to understand. Then she clutched Róisín's hands and Onion's thighs, and walked out onto the beam, heading for the other pole. Onion groaned as he felt the metal frame beneath him move under their weight. Bucket appeared on the second pole ahead of them, coming up with almost as much agility as Maya.

Onion and the two apes were trapped. There was nowhere to go.

CHAPTER TWENTY-EIGHT:
—
TYPICAL

Down below, the Michaels had arrived with the rest of the Five O's. Getting out of the truck, they could see Maya, visible to the whole of Ballinlud, scaling past all the cables on one of the four centre poles of the Big Top and Truck and Bucket climbing after her. It took another moment to realise Maya was carrying Róisín.

And Onion. She had Onion up there too.

'This is just typical of him,' Sive said, shaking her head and rolling her eyes. 'Just typical!'

Forester had the back of the van open and had taken out three drones. Using his phone, he switched them on and sent them flying into the air. Then he ran in to the Big Top and disappeared. Major Michaels jumped out of the car and sprinted after him, with Sive close behind. Derek, Dallan and Clíona got out of the car and watched as the remote-control aircraft rose up in formation. Forester was clearly controlling the drones from wherever he was hiding, guiding them up towards Maya at the top of the tent.

'He's going to use the drones to try and knock them off!' Dallan gasped.

'He's caught and he knows it,' Michelle Michaels said from behind them. 'He's finished. The guards will close his circus down for this. Now, he's just out for revenge. We have to stop him before he hurts those poor orang-utans!' Then she added. 'And Onion!'

CHAPTER TWENTY-EIGHT: TYPICAL

Luckily, most of the other circus workers weren't getting involved. It seemed things had gone too far for them. Keeping a couple of orang-utans secret was one thing. Endangering kids was another thing entirely. And now the apes had been seen out in the open, they knew the game was up. Police sirens were sounding in the distance. The guards were on their way, though it might be too late for Onion and the apes. Some of the circus people were already running for the few trucks and vans that were parked nearby.

'Clíona, do you think you could hack into those drones and use them against Truck and Bucket?' Dallan asked.

'No,' Clíona said, holding out her empty hands. 'I can't do that. We're not in a *Mission Impossible* film. Even if I had, y'know, a computer. Or my phone.' She pointed to Róisín, high up on the Big Top. The ape still had the phone on a cord around her neck.

'Yeah, and I've got no credit,' Derek said hurriedly, before Clíona could start doing weird things to *his* phone.

Sive came running back out of the tent. 'We've found Forester,' she told them, breathing fast around her chewing gum. 'But there's a problem.'

They followed her in and saw what she was talking about. Major Michaels was in the middle of the ring, between all four centre poles, staring almost straight up into the air. Forester was sitting in a sling, hanging from one of the brackets set up for the trapeze, ten metres high and out in the big open space in the roof of the tent. He'd pulled up the only rope ladder. There was no way to reach him.

'Do you think there's anything round here we can poke him with?' Derek asked.

'Derek!' Clíona exclaimed.

'Nothing sharp or anything – just something to make him get down.'

CHAPTER TWENTY-EIGHT: TYPICAL

Forester knew the guards would get him eventually, but for now, there was no way of stopping him from using those drones. He glared down at the Five O's and their primatologist friends and laughed in a way that sounded like he was going slightly crazy, which was very possible.

'There'll be ladders outside for taking down the tent,' said Major Michaels. 'You, boy! Get the ladder,' he ordered.

'But I'm a girl,' answered Sive.

'Whatever. Boys, girls, all the same to me. Now retrieve the ladder and build a pile of stuff high enough to position the ladder against it at a 60 degree angle. If we can get high enough, we will be able to reach him.'

Derek stared hard up at the ringmaster, and he nodded to the other Five O's. 'Let's do it,' he said in a grim voice. 'Nobody messes with my brother but me.'

And so, they started grabbing whatever they could find that was heavy and solid enough to make a pile they could lean a ladder against. The clown car was there, and they started with that, piling on boxes, stage gear and whatever else they could find. Every now and then, Derek stopped to throw juggling balls and skittles at Forester, who laughed down at him like a maniac.

Clíona stood back from it all, gazing at the growing pile of random objects, at the ringmaster above it and the ropes, struts and pulleys that criss-crossed the space above her. This was taking too long. They weren't going to be in time.

CHAPTER TWENTY-NINE:
—
AIRBORNE

U p on the Big Top, Onion was dragging breaths into lungs that were on the point of collapse. Maya had put him down, and he was hugging the latticed frame of the beam, afraid to move, afraid to stay still, afraid to look down, afraid to keep his eyes open, afraid to close his eyes and, generally speaking, just very, very afraid. In fact, his brain was so jangled by fear that he almost didn't feel any fear at all because his mind was a roar of white noise and he couldn't think any more and any time now he was just going to pass out and be done with all this madness.

He and Maya and Róisín were all out in the middle of the metal beam, high above everything else around them, with Truck crawling in from one end and Bucket edging in from the other. The giant clown was unsteady, moving forward on hands and knees. The trapeze artist was completely comfortable, up on his feet and nearly within reach of Maya, with the catch pole tucked under one arm. He was signing to her, a pleading expression on his face, telling her he didn't want to hurt anyone: he just wanted things to go back to the way they were. He kept reassuring her as he came forward, then he gave up and took hold of the catch pole again.

Something buzzed past Onion, giving him such a fright he nearly fell off the beam, and he screamed. Looking out after it, he saw it was a drone. Two more were flying in circles around them, taking turns to dart in and around Maya. She stood protectively over Róisín on the beam, watching them and swiping at them when they came in too close.

CHAPTER TWENTY-NINE: AIRBORNE

They're going to knock her off, Onion thought, and it was a miracle he could put even that thought together. They'll knock her off and she'll fall.

That seemed to be the intention. The three little aircraft, each one the size of a dinner plate, were zipping around the orang-utan, tormenting her as she tried to keep them away from her child. Róisín gazed pleadingly at Onion, who dearly wanted to help, but fear had attached him to that beam firmer than a gargoyle to a wall. As Maya was being distracted, Bucket was inching closer to her, the catch pole held ready in his hands.

Down below, Onion saw the other Five O's heading into the tent – Sive and some outdoorsy guy first, then the others and some outdoorsy woman. The people from the wildlife park. They'd come to take Róisín and Maya away. Even if he got out of this alive, he'd probably never see the two apes again. He closed his eyes and sniffed back a sob.

Onion was so caught up in what was happening below, he'd forgotten about Truck. He sensed a shadow fall over him and twisted round to see the powerlifting clown reaching out to grab his arm. He flinched and pulled away, nearly

losing his grip. Truck cursed, steadied herself and reached for him again. Onion moved back, right up against Róisín, who was clinging to Maya's leg, frightened by the drones.

'LEAVE THEM ALONE!' Onion shrieked. 'WHY CAN'T YOU JUST LEAVE THEM ALONE?'

Truck was beyond reasoning. The secret of The Great Orangini was out, and she and her boss were probably going to prison. The guards were on their way. All that was left to her was revenge. And if this stringy kid got in her way, that was just too bad.

A drone smacked into Maya and she let out a yelp, nearly losing her balance. Another one came buzzing in towards Róisín, and Onion lunged out to slap at it, the delicate, blurred rotors stinging his fingers. It spun away and crashed against the centre pole.

And Onion lost his balance and tipped forward off the beam.

He had a moment of clarity, when he hoped his granny couldn't see this because she'd kill him, and then he fell. It all seemed to happen very slowly. His arms and legs thrashed as he tried to snatch at empty air. Then he saw Maya grip the beam with her feet, saw her swing out and down, her long arms stretching out, strong fingers grasping for his . . .

And . . . SHE MISSED! And he kept falling.

'OW!' he cried, as he felt a sharp pain in his left ankle and something pulled him up short, his glasses fell off and his inhaler hit him in the eye. Pure animal reflex made him catch his glasses, because the animal in him was still more concerned about Granny giving out to him for breaking his glasses than it was about dying.

Putting the specs back on, he peered up past his feet and saw Bucket hanging off the beam with one hand, the other holding the catch pole. The loop of the pole was wrapped tight around Onion's ankle. The trapeze artist hauled him up and dragged him onto the beam. Onion took a breath of his inhaler before his lungs seized up altogether, then he shifted round to look at Forester's henchman, who was still holding him steady.

Bucket nodded towards the two apes, who were still being tormented by the drones as Maya tried to hold off Truck. Bucket, who hadn't said a word for the entire time, suddenly said, 'I'm sorry' … in the highest, squeakiest voice Onion had ever heard. He sounded like he'd swallowed one of Róisín's squeaky toys. Even though he was in great danger, Onion almost laughed. It's no wonder the trapeze artist chose to keep quiet. His high-pitched voice made him a lot less menacing.

'Sure, sure. But . . . can you get us down from here, please?'

CHAPTER THIRTY:
—
SHOWMANSHIP

Inside the Big Top, the pile of objects they were building to lean the ladder on was getting increasingly desperate. It was tall, nearly big enough to brace the ladder against, but it wasn't getting any taller. The more stuff they added to it, the more fell off. Major Michaels was now thrusting the ladder up, trying to poke at Forester, who was kicking the top of it away and cackling, then going back to controlling the drones on his phone.

Clíona was still standing off to one side, staring up at the roof of the tent.

'You could try helping, you know!' Sive shouted over.

CHAPTER THIRTY: SHOWMANSHIP

'I am helping!' Clíona called back.

Her eyes were following the cable that held Forester's sling, up to the bracket, through that frame, along the strut, getting mixed in with a bunch of other cables . . .

Derek was cursing now, telling the two adults to hold the ladder against the heap of stage gear, hoping they could keep it steady enough for him to climb up. Michelle Michaels tried to stop him, saying it should be her who climbed up, but Derek didn't wait. He started up the ladder as everyone else tried to hold it still. The pile was shaky, and the ladder swayed and twisted. Derek clung to the rungs, teeth gritted as he climbed.

'You think you can take me in my own Big Top?' Forester roared down at them, his thumbs steering the two remaining drones around above him, and he watched with glee through their cameras as his attacks wore Maya down, smacking into her time after time. 'This is my place! My world! My natural habitat!'

Clíona's eyes traced the cable along another strut, through a pulley, down to a post where it and a load of other cables were tied off. Walking over, she counted off the hooks they were knotted to, reached in and took hold of the end of the right cable. Then she yanked it off its hook.

'Look at you!' Forester was screeching contemptuously at those below him. 'You're ridiculous! COME AND GET ME, YOU LOSERS! COME AND GE—'

Then the sling that was holding him snapped loose and he dropped like a rock. Plummeting past Derek, who was wobbling at the top of the ladder, Forester crashed down through the pile of boxes and packing cases, smashed through the roof of the clown car and thudded into the back seat. Confetti flew everywhere, the little car burst into pieces, the horn giving off a loud 'PARP', and then the remains of the car died with a sad, squeaky wheeze.

Derek found himself at the top of a ladder that was no longer leaning against anything. He

wailed as the others tried to slow the fall of the ladder, with little success. Forester, saved from the worst of his fall by the stunt car, was getting to his feet when the ladder slammed down on top of him and Derek tumbled off the end of it. The ringmaster pulled free, badly dazed, and tried one more time to get his feet, staggering around.

'Did you see that, Bridie?' The Ferg said to his partner from where they'd appeared at the entrance to the tent. 'What flair the man has! What timing! He's a born showman! He's a genius! He's—'

'He's under arrest,' Garda Judge declared.

Forester saw the guards and turned to stumble away towards the back of the tent, but Major Michaels swung a fist into his jaw and flattened him.

Dallan found the ringmaster's phone in the wreckage of the clown car and looked at the views offered by the drones' cameras. Bucket had let the apes go past him. They were on their way down. Bucket was carrying Onion, who was as white as toothpaste. Truck was coming down after them, though her climbing skills were no match for the orang-utans or the trapeze artist. By the time she got down, they were running to the other guards who were striding towards the circus.

Truck saw the police and stopped in her tracks. She spun around and started running in the other direction, behind the Big Top. From somewhere near the back of the tent, the Five O's heard a hard girl's voice: 'Lads, take 'er down!'

Truck was just passing an open flap of the tent when the Bang-Off-Them Brothers charged into her, shoulders to her belly, flipping her into the air and dropping her smack on her back, badly winded. By the time she'd regained her senses enough to try and get up, Garda Judge had jumped on her, got her in an armlock and snapped handcuffs on her.

Tina stood over the powerlifting clown and snorted. 'Yeah, that's what I thought. You tell Forester he can call me when he's ready to play in the big leagues. I don't work with amateurs.'

The Ferg was cuffing Forester, an expression of bitter betrayal on the guard's face. 'I'm so disappointed in you, Joe,' he said in what was almost a sob. 'I looked up to you. But stealing orang-utans? Lying to your public? Endangering kids? Whatever happened to living for the love of the show? Whatever happened to the Clown's Code of Honour, Joe?'

'Garda, show some pity on an old man,' Forester growled to Bridie Judge as she walked past with Truck. 'Put me in prison so I don't have to listen to this fool's nonsense any longer. I'm done!'

CHAPTER THIRTY-ONE:

GOING HOME

Tina Dalton was talking to Róisín.

'It was a privilege to play ball with you,' she said earnestly, shaking the ape's hand. 'You're a joy to watch on the court. If you ever fancy cutting free from these losers, you give me a call. You'll do that, won't you? You'll give me a call?'

She did the phone gesture with her hand to the side of her head as she backed away, then she tossed her head to the twins and they walked off.

Róisín was standing next to Onion, leaning against his leg. Maya was sitting close by, munching through a bag of bananas the Michaels had given her. The guards were rounding up what was left of the circus people, and Bucket was with The Ferg and Judge. Bucket was giving his statement in his high-pitched tone, The Ferg and Judge trying not to laugh. Bucket told them he was ashamed of what had happened to Onion and the apes. He loved the circus and he loved Maya and Róisín, and he was finished with all the lying. He was willing to tell the whole story, even if he sounded like a bag of cats who'd swallowed a can of helium while he was telling it.

The Five O's were gathered next to the Michaels' SUV. The primatologists were getting ready to take the apes home to Tota Freedom Wildlife Park, which was down the far end of Wicklow. The gang were all upset to see the orang-utans go, but Onion in particular was heartbroken. He got down on his knees and hugged Róisín to him.

'We're very grateful for everything you've done,' Michelle was saying. 'Mike and I would like to offer all of you lifetime membership of the park. You'll be welcome to come any time you like! Maya is a dear friend to us. Losing her hit us hard, and we've missed her so much. We're so happy to have her back, and delighted that we have Róisín now too. They both deserve a decent home, and they have it now, thanks to you.'

Onion nodded sadly and kissed Róisín on the top of her head and let her go. Sive hurried over to see them off as the young ape took her mother's hand and they climbed into the back seat of the car. Major Michaels buckled them in and then came back to shake each of the kids' hands.

'Thank you again, children,' he said. 'I hope you'll come and see us all soon, and by soon I mean sixteen hundred hours on Tuesdays or weekends at approximately oh-nine hundred.'

Tears welled once more in Onion's eyes as the car drove away. Derek put an arm around his shoulders and gave him a quick hug, and then a dead arm just in case anyone was looking and thought he was in their stupid gang. Sive was more sincere and wrapped her arms around both of them, then Dallan and Clíona did the same.

Pulling apart, the five kids turned to look up at the Big Top, still trying to get their heads around everything that had happened.

'That was pretty mad, wasn't it?' Onion said in a shaky voice.

'Yes,' Sive agreed. 'Yes, it was. Let's never do anything like that again.'

CHAPTER THIRTY-ONE: GOING HOME

They were all quiet for a minute, each one lost in their own thoughts.

Then: 'Aw, man!' Derek gasped, looking at the time on his phone. 'Onion, we're late for dinner. Granny's gonna kill us!'

And with that, the two boys set off running for home and, just maybe, a bit of normal life for a while.